## ❧ *The Body* ❧

By the same author:

FIREMAN FLOWER
THREE

# THE BODY

## William Sansom

HARCOURT, BRACE AND COMPANY    NEW YORK

*The Body*

# 1

To hold the syringe gently, firmly but delicately—not to squirt, but to prod the sleeper into wakefulness with the nozzle, taking care to start no abrupt flight of fear. Only to stir a movement, to initiate a presence from such a deep dead sleep. Gently, gently—lean thus into the ivy, face close in to the leaves, bowed in yet hardly daring to breathe, not to shake a single leaf, hand held far away up the wall, but face now close, secret, smelling the earth underneath the ivy like a smell close to earlier days, intimate the eyes and closed the world . . . then carefully prod, no, tickle—tickle the long dead leg on the leaf.

But still this curious fly slept on. I bent closer, risking a cramp, tautening round the brass syringe my pale, large-looking fingers. Somewhere overhead was the afternoon, spread out wide and calm; there was a pale clear May sky overhead. Four o'clock the hour—the edge-hour before tea. No one about. People everywhere resting. So that down by the ivy I was secure, nothing to disturb the secret moment.

That squat syringe filled with brown glutinous killer armed me powerfully; still—it was forbidden, naughty to

play with flies, embarrassing for an adult to be uncovered
at such play. It had thus to be done quickly, before anyone saw. Yet this perverse fly remained fast asleep! It
might be dead already! There on the dark ivy leaf how
still, its long leather-jacket legs firmly hooked into place.
Envigored with insect stealth? Drugged with a wealth of
parturition? Its red head bowed, its long cigar body
tapering away into the mysterious hairlike sting. So
deep a sleep was dangerous, an unnatural sleep with
sharp-beaked birds perched searching on every tree? But
precious time was passing, I nudged the leaf with the
nozzle. The whole ivy shook—such a shaking at human
level would have meant an earthquake, an upturning of
houses and a crumbling of lives. Yet the fly's hooked
limbs remained set; though now, as the leaf shook again
still, as if in afterthought like a disturbed sleeper it
ambled its legs up, staggered drunkenly—and subsided
again into position. Its legs stretched out still again like
exhausted pistons. Close there to the leaves, with the
world contracted and all things small made huge as in
the first world of private garden games, I could see the
gothic melancholy of last year's cobwebs hung with mor-
tar dust on the dark wall underneath the ivy. A fearful
place—but the dragon slept unmoved in such forest quiet,
in the faint luminous mixture of shade and reflected sunlight. Then huge, bullying, godlike, I drew back the piston
of the syringe.

Suddenly the air above clapped loud with sound, sound
from the grown-up afternoon above. I stopped, half
straightened myself, looked round and up to the windows
of my house. Instantly again a land of light, of wide blue
sky! I saw silhouetted the towered shape of the house,
my home, that stood a hundred feet back from where I

stood. Close by, separated by a few yards that formed
a sort of well laid with tradesmen's entrances and sheds,
stood my neighbor's house. The noise had come echoing
from this well, the asphalt place between houses. It was
the sound, loud and abrupt, that breaks still afternoons
with the prelude of tea and new movement—the ringing
rushing of water in the landing lavatory and the gurgling
freshness of water in the basin. A bathroom echo, footsteps and a banging of doors—the siesta received in its
face a splash of water. No more the heavy-breathed
sleeping, no more soft light through curtains and blinds
and shutters. Now the patting of beds, the bustling of
feet downstairs, the clattering of teacups in kitchens clean
and washed from lunch. I knew that my wife had risen
from sleep.

But then—half-bent and alert, hand still on the drawn-
out piston handle—I caught sight of something that kept
me there: something that made me suddenly blush with
anger. It was a head across the wall, a head no more than
a few feet from mine, yet in the garden stealth unaware
of my own silent presence. I saw it through the creepered
trellis topping the wall: the young leaves masked my face
perfectly, leaves of a bird-watcher's bonnet; I could see
without being seen.

A face—full, red, with bluish lips and a heavy ginger
mustache.

But what angered me was its direction: it was staring
straight up at the bathroom window where my wife was
making such fresh sounds of washing. I knew that Madge
would be wearing no more than a slip—if that. And those
bluish lips had curled open and were hung in an open-
mouthed smile, the small pig's eyes had disappeared into
themselves roguishly, all the man's head was poked un-

ashamedly forward, hungrily, eating with its mouth whatever fleeting movements were passing above where the
frosted window stuck out open.

Quite suddenly—almost as if some shadow of guilt had
tapped him on the shoulder—suddenly the stranger
glanced slyly to the left up the wall, and then round so
that his eyes seemed to stare straight into mine. I held
myself stiller than before, horrified to be found watching
this watching man. His eyes stayed for a fixed second—
then swiveled back to the window. At the same time he
moved a pace to one side, perhaps the better to see—but
perhaps to hide himself behind some projection of creeper?
And had the creeper hidden me? Had he actually seen
me—and simply not cared? And—who was he anyhow?
A tradesman? A guest next door? A wanderer into empty
afternoon houses, a housebreaker? I was almost boiling
up the courage, the aggression to shout over and ask the
fellow what confounded tricks he thought he was up to—
when the frosted window above suddenly banged itself
shut!

Then, as a further muffled bang closed the bathroom
door and finalized the exit of whatever picture had presented itself, the stranger's face dropped abruptly blank.
For a moment he continued to stare up at the frosted
barricade: and then out broke the ginger smile again;
he wagged his head from side to side in what looked like
gluttonous memory at such luck, and suddenly shuffled his
arms and legs up and down in a clumsy step-dance—then
gathered himself together and blew a kiss to the window.
He wiped the back of his hand across his mouth as if to
disguise the kiss—and as if someone were looking—turned
on his heel and was gone. A back door banged.

I stood for a moment shocked by this sudden exit. The

situation was closed—but unanswered. Then, just then, a new anxiety flashed up in my mind. Was that kiss the first? Was the man perhaps in the habit of blowing kisses to the window? Had Madge been smiling down at him? Was I—after so many years—waking up to some unbelievable play conducted habitually behind my back?

It must have been at this moment that the first suspicions began to wriggle out their short, apprehensive roots. How greedy for sustenance they were may not have depended as much on the ginger man as upon other matters. I am no seeker of innuendo, I think I am at most times a quiet man—indeed usually I am sure I would have been levelheaded enough to dismiss objectively the whole episode as a contemptible small impertinence. But that afternoon for some reason I was flustered by a confusion beyond my control. A sudden onrush of strong emotions; self-pity, envy, guilt and common anger rose at this affront. Pity for myself, for being excluded from what concerned Madge, from what was rightfully mine; envy, I am sure, of this mustached intruder's virile appearance; guilt that I had failed to assert myself and attack him; anger at such a successful breaching of dignity and position. And I remember one other curious feeling—I had no thought of sympathy for Madge, no sympathy for her privacy outraged: instead, surprisingly, I assumed her collaboration. Yet never before in our twenty years of marriage can I remember seriously distrusting her.

I remember giving the syringe a short jab, plunging in the vicious handle—and squirting all over that quiescent fly a stream of thick, brown, oily liquid. The ivy leaves all round were spattered, drenched, dripped long gelatinous threads. The fly staggered, gathered its legs up like a spindly tractor, threshed out once, pulled off a

leg, and subsided stuck and shivering weakly. I remember
that—but then I lost interest. At another time I would
have noted carefully the insect's reaction—rather playing the biologist. But I saw nothing—except a vision
against the ivy of the ginger head, and my wife's figure
framed in frosted glass. It was a terrible thing that another man should see her so.

—Tea!

I jerked up abruptly, looked round to see Madge standing by the conservatory door. She had changed her dress
and now stood washed-looking in a pale summer dress.
She showed her arms bare to the middle of round pink
washed biceps. She patted the back of her bleached hair
impatiently:

—Henry, don't you want your tea?

—Eh?

—It's been waiting twenty minutes. I've been down ten
minutes myself.

A lie?

—Taking a look at this ivy, dear. Strangling everything.

—Strangling the wall? How can it do that? Now do
come in and have your tea, it's getting cold.

I was just going to answer, when a resounding jangle
came from the kitchen bell, and with it a bursting-open
clatter of the side door. Footsteps echoed in the passage,
someone kicked a dustbin. Madge called:

—Who's there? Who is it?

And abruptly a face poked itself round the trellis that
screened the passage—that face with a ginger mustache!

—I say, I'm awfully sorry.

I heard my wife saying absurdly—curiously: 'Do you
want anything?'

And then the stranger came into the garden. I cannot

say 'calmly,' he made a sudden sprinting jump over a
narrow bed of small flowers—it was meant to be comic—
and then stood hands in trouser pockets, straining his
neck back at the flower bed and then suddenly looking up
with his chin stuck out and his small blue eyes staring
straight at Madge. Then at me.

–I say, I hope I haven't disturbed you, have I?

He was drawling, revolving his chin and drawing in
efficient breaths through his lower teeth.

–But you're right. I do want something. Ah, you were
right there, dear lady!

He broke into laughter, then stopped. He bowed to
Madge, and touched an imaginary cap peak to me. It was
appalling. Then suddenly his manner changed absolutely,
he leaned forward twisting his mustache painfully and
whispering in a tone of most secluded confidence:

–I want to borrow a screw driver.

There was a brief pause while this man looked from
Madge to me and back twice—moving his head sharply
to and fro—and then just as Madge was opening her
mouth, he was speaking again. This time the words
streamed out in a tirade, and at the same time he kept
pointing to the house next door.

–But allow me to introduce myself—Charles Suffolk
Diver. Address: Number 48. Next door to yours. And if
you'd believe it, neither our esteemed hostess nor one of
her eleven worthy guests can produce among them such
an article as the humble screw driver. A practical lot, you
might say? You'd be right—far from it. And so I says
to myself I says: 'Charles Diver, there's only one thing
for it—try your neighbor.' And here I am, making the
proverbial nuisance of myself!

He gave a final chuckle, screwed up his face with a

Yet that day they returned with astounding definition, to my envious eyes pristine. What thus approached with the screw driver might be likened to an abstract figure of memory—a face, two feet, a pale dress held together by agencies unseen.

–Dear lady, a thousand thanks!

His eyes glinted expertly over the screw driver, yet his lips puckered in a smile:

–You've saved my life.

–Oh, not at all.

For a few minutes more they chatted. Pleasantries were exchanged, the fact of new neighborhood asserted and confirmed. Charles Diver made several jokes, which Madge applauded with bursts of high hysterical laughter—it seemed once, I think even to her, that she would never stop, for finally she placed her whole hand across her mouth and leaned her body over a garden chair. As for me, I was hot with irritation, my brain itself seemed to be blushing—though I retained myself sufficiently to make now and then a polite noise. At the jokes I think I must have stretched my lips like a man who has run his tongue along the metal of an electric battery.

Then at last, brandishing the screw driver and in fact making several passes with it as though it were some sort of a cutlass, Diver turned to go. I began my sigh of relief —only to stop short as fatally that fellow paused before his return jump over the flower bed. He turned and delivered straight at me his annihilating broadside:

–I say. I hardly want to sound precipitous. But perhaps, now we're neighbors and all that, perhaps you and Mrs. Bishop would honor me at my humble abode one night?

The names of days—Monday, Tuesday, Friday—

erected themselves instantly in front of my eyes. I was
ready to counter each one of them. But Diver had
already seen my mouth opening. He laughed.

–No no no. I won't take no for an answer.

And then, to the skies, the garden, the houses:

–It simply doesn't matter *when*. Any night you like—
name your day! There—what could be fairer than that?

Wild speculations of a false holiday, a business trip,
filmed themselves across my private eye. I saw the promenade at Eastbourne quite clearly. But Madge was already saying:

–Saturday—what's wrong with Saturday?

She burst with laughter.

And Diver pealed back.

–I should think there's everything *right* about Saturday.

Madge burst again at this, she threw her pretty head
back like a blond painted mule. The bray petered to a
titter and then she said with some emphasis:

–Well, *Henry* and *I* would *love* to come.

It was done. Diver bowed solemnly, waved the screw
driver once more, and skipped off over the flowers. He
called back 'Saturday!' from the well between the houses:
and the word echoed in that hollow place like a medieval
challenge. It resounded as large as an unaccountable
weight of blood clouding my forehead. I remember that
even through these irritations I shook my head and told
myself not to be an old fool. But as instantly a wave of
indignation again rose, dramatizing itself, becoming right-
ful anger at such an intrusion on my privacy: couldn't
a man have two square yards of his own without being
pestered by strangers?

Madge was patting the back of her golden hair—her

hand should have come away coated with a fine gold dust, the dust of crushed beetle wings—and straightening the front of her dress:

—Such a nice man. So cheery. And a gentleman.

—Hm.

—I suppose he must have bought the garage past the Parade. I wonder how long he's been living there?

—Hm.

—Henry, what are all these 'hms'? You look as though you've swallowed the parson's nose. Don't you like Mr. Diver?

The direct assault. At all costs this had to be deflected. I said:

—It's not, my dear, a question of liking or disliking. I really have no particular feelings about Mr. Diver. But if *that's* the way to borrow a screw driver, then I'm a . . . Not that I mind anyone borrowing my screw driver—on the contrary I'm *glad* to be of help. But when it comes to listening to a concert party, seeing the flower beds trampled, being intruded upon right and left in my own garden, and finally having to dine with a fellow I don't know from Adam—then I draw the line, my dear, and I think I'm . . .

—But, Henry—he didn't trample any flower beds. . . .

—Hm. Well. You seem pretty interested anyhow.

At this Madge opened her eyes very wide, she turned their full blue surprise straight on me. She studied me for a moment closely and at the same time a smile of rare delight came over her face—bringing into abrupt definition the deep dimples, stretching the lips out and up in a crescent so that even the smallest back teeth were disclosed suddenly in the sun. And she said, using with love and wonder a word from a private vocabulary we had:

—Oh! *Boocles!*

## 2

It was five o'clock. I remember pausing for a long time by the cash till before leaving my shop. I dithered about—going over to the showcase and looking at the bottles of lotion and the tortoise-shell combs, at the backs of wax heads and their wigs staring out to the street, at the cream-fringed blinds round the window. Then I went back to the cash till—not to ask a question of the cashier, nor to see myself as often I did in the mirror behind the cashier's desk, but simply to linger as long as possible before leaving for the afternoon. I wanted any excuse to stay. Usually in business one can find many such imaginary excuses—but that day my mind was too concerned to invent them. It was Saturday. I was due to dine with Charles Diver.

At length it was the cashier herself who sent me off. I grew conscious that she was beginning to fidget, to scribble too hard in her ledger—and recognizing that this was only a mirror of my own condition I hurried out. The doorbell rang its bright welcome behind me with the snap of a circus whip.

Out onto the gray pavement of Seychelles Parade,

thence to the rich desuetudes of those avenues that led me homewards. A decaying place, but one for which ordinarily I had a deep affection. I liked the generous romantic villas of so many different kinds: old and peeling their tired stucco; or creeper-grown and grim in brownish London brick; or dull and deadly still when suddenly they showed bare some pile of Moorish and gothic and Italianate towers and porches and balconies. Portly shells from the spacious days, they stood back with some discretion from the plane-treed avenues; and in their gardens there grew the full luxuriance of blossoming shrubs and trees planted seventy or eighty years before. Such avenues hold a pleasant damp smell of roots, of underbrush—and the houses themselves give each year a little of their basement brick to the mothering earth.

That day, chestnut blossoms had fallen and lay silted like confetti round the drains. Few people were about. A street sweeper wheeled along his little dustbin; a milk cart with bottles ringing wandered its orange color against the tree trunks and the weathered walls beyond; two cars swirled through and disappeared, leaving a clean glint of silver; over one front door a striped sunblind stirred its hot folds of shade as someone sounded a doorbell. There was a prescience of summer in the air, the calm spring sky stood high and hazed, tinged with yellow, so that it appeared like the sky of a southern painting. Trees and roofs stood out against it warmly dead, with Italian immobility, not alive but cast in oil and dark glass. Wherever a black object touched the sky—a sooted chimney, a dark turret—one remembered the funereal south of cypress and misericordia.

But that day I got no pleasure from this accustomed walk. I was angry. If at times I looked up and saw what

I remember so clearly now, it must have been the result of feeling very much alone—as I think one often sees things most clearly in moments of exclusion; as, when people fail, one turns for solace to things. But mostly I felt angry, indignant still at what I had seen a few days before, doubly indignant at having to face at dinner the object of my indignation. So that a black hood of self kept falling over me, I walked along like a slow engine obsessed with the fire burning up inside, conscious only of the pavement a few yards ahead. Yet that is perhaps a little strong—it suggests the anger of an obsessed introvert always indulging in pains and ills of his own exaggeration. I do not think—even after all that has since passed—that I am that. In fact I would say the opposite—a man of very small passion. Ordinary, from ordinary middle-class beginnings, and if at all extraordinary then in the mildest and safest way—I am what is called a little 'old-fashioned.'

I suppose, too, I do have my small obsessions. Since this account is a kind of confessional—certainly it is no journal, nor a disinterested history, but rather an attempt to get out onto paper feelings and events which have worried me deeply, which still worry me—since it is this, then I must take pains to be fair. For instance, I have described my wife unkindly. This is not because I did not love her then, but because I do not believe love casts any permanent film of illusion over the eyes. Quite often I have looked at Madge most dispassionately, and found her face not only uninteresting but actively unpleasant: yet I believe that in those moments a deeper chord of affection still played. And certainly a few minutes later I would feel only affection and love. Together we passed what I think is one of the greatest tests of love—we felt a real sensation of tolerance and pleasure when one of us did something against the other's principles. It is absurd, as another but purely physical proposition, to love a varicose vein: Madge has some of these, and while I cannot pretend not to see them at one time or another, I disregard them—and feel a tenderness, almost a conspiratorial tenderness, when she who would dearly love the thinnest silk stockings instead chooses thick ones; or on at least one occasion wore two pairs of thin. So if now I seem to speak harshly of her, it is an attempt to recapture the feeling of a time when suddenly, for the first time, I felt alien from her. And looked at her with distrust: though at the same time I wanted her so much.

I must be equally fair and confess myself probably rather a dull man. It annoys her, I know, that at week ends I wear old-fashioned tweed knickerbockers and stockings. I am sure she would rather I was more athletic, and that I had not a jumpy way of walking on my toes. She would prefer my amusements to be more modern—the cinema, bridge, sport. But I am essentially a man left over from the home-hobby age, a man unconditioned to the stadium. Only forty-five, but my sympathies are with the time when men and women sweated over commons with butterfly nets. It seems to me that the end was more interesting, more instructive than the destination of a ball. Though I do not nowadays chase butterflies, my favorite occupation is a sort of botanizing—and this and its atmosphere must be very dull for Madge. I read a lot, if irregularly; and I like very much to browse among my father's scientific volumes. I like—let it be stated honestly—the tale of the development of the steam engine, the dramatic Victorian presentation of the lava flows of Vesuvius, of the mighty kraken, of geysers on North

Island and of Edison's achievement. There is a certain solidity, a certainty, a diligent sense of inquiry that I find missing in life nowadays. These, then, are my obsessions. But everyone has some obsession. An obsession can be no more than a mental preoccupation out of proportion with the reality of daily life (and how is one to decide exactly what that reality is?). The housewife's tale of a neighbor, the sportsman's talk of his ball, the drinker's recounting of his drinks—all are obsessive and the mind behind them might as well be revolving in space.

On the whole, I should think my so-called obsessions are more annoying to me than to anyone else. The truth is, I am not good at them. I plan, but do not act. Sometimes I plan days to read up this or that subject thoroughly— so that I may acquire definitive *knowledge*—and then after an hour put the book down—usually with some excuse, a broken chair to mend, some fresh air to get. Or I skip several hundred pages and alight on a very different subject, which I begin reading with new wonder which in its own turn soon declines. All this with an irritating tenseness of guilt. It is the same feeling as reading a newspaper and, even at a moment of breath-taking climax, letting the eye wander to some smaller item. However, I persist. And I suppose I act like most men—carrying to the grave their unfulfilled dreams, promising themselves with a never-failing reserve of hope that 'one day' they will fulfill them. Perhaps it is, at any rate, the hope that counts.

Not that I am at all hindered in my material life— that cannot be said, it is the opposite. Since my parents died, I have been left both a large old-fashioned house and the near-by family business. The business—a court hairdresser's established in the last century—runs itself: it has seen its best days in the prosperity of the newly built suburb, but I still draw a comfortable income, and there is a modern branch towards the West End. I was trained in the business, and even now in a general way I superintend it. But it is ably managed; I call in for a few hours only each day, and only lend a practical hand when some unusual matter calls—a particular type of *postiche*, a seborrhea scare. However, even this minor call on my time does little to disturb me—the shop itself has a pleasing air of another decade. And it stands with others back in a small Parade far from the main roads, a sort of village among the Victorian terraces stretching everywhere around. Nothing disturbs a tired, kind of dying, peace. All old shops: the Italian Warehouseman, his name friezed in curling gold letters on chipped black glass; the ironmonger, crowned with plaster oil pots flourishing a red and green script announcing 'Linseed and Colza Oils'; the glazed tiles and black hooks of the Butcher and Grazier; the Ladies' Draper, with its low glass window sleekly bound in brass and its whitely musty profusion of small clothes; the Pharmaceutical Chemist gleaming with rows of gilt bottles shelved into the darkness within. And so on—all old-fashioned concerns with no discordant note. And so too my own house—which in these times is half shut up—a lumbering pile turreted like a French château, extravagant but grown to be homely, and standing now almost exactly as it stood in my father's day. He indeed must have had some effect on me—he would allow nothing to be changed.

So altogether a passive, passionless life. It had its upsets from time to time, but neither Madge nor I took them very seriously, and with our different interests and our deep affection we managed to get along comfortably and in a modest way quite happily. Yet—for some reason

that I find impossible to define—on that Saturday I had
suddenly become nervous and irritated as I can never remember before. As I said, I took little interest in the
walk home that customarily I enjoyed. The black hood
of self kept falling down, as it were palpably on my forehead. I felt a muttering twitch at my lips: stopped it:
then found it beginning again a few steps later. I was
making resolutions, imagining scenes. My mind, and sometimes my lips, said to myself: I'll have to speak to the
fellow—tell him who's who. Politely, as man to man.
Or . . . with dignity, cold dignity. Before dinner? Take
him aside afterwards? One could begin casually, hands
in pockets. 'Er—Diver, a little matter I've been wanting
to have a chat about.' And then something impersonal,
said gravely, with at the end a sudden cock of the eyes
straight at him, 'My wife and I have been married now
for twenty years. A fine woman, Mrs. Bishop. Popular
with everybody—and respected. Good company, good fun.
But what I will say is, she knows where to draw the line.
Never exceeds herself like some: never a word out of place.
No man respects her more than I—no woman respects
her more than she respects herself.'

I saw the frown on my own forehead, and then the slight
pallor across Diver's red face. Diver drew himself up, and
after a brief pause, spoke, staring straight in front of
him. He spoke very quietly, 'I quite understand, sir.' And
then the two of us exchanged a meaning look—and returned to the company. And all this occurred—curiously
—in a room owned by an aunt of mine, a room with French
windows, a budgerigar's cage placed on a wicker table,
a pot of ferns. It was at the yellowing ends of these ferns
that Diver had looked with such intensity.

I had turned out of Seychelles Parade and was walking

along a crescent of regular stuccoed villas. Their high
windows reflected darkly the trees and clouds. Black and
white tiled steps led up to each regular porch.

Suddenly, shockingly, I saw Diver's face again. But
this time it never paled, instead it grew redder, the mustache stiffened, and a long leering smile opened his lips
and crept along the teeth as though it would never end.
To my horror he slapped me on the back and said, distinctly: 'Bob's your uncle!' And winked.

What did this mean? The phrase assumed a cabalistic
mystery, it whirred in and out of my brain like a strip of
illuminated letters. 'All right,' I said to myself, 'if he
wants a scene, he'll have one.' And other visions presented
themselves. I was rising suddenly to my feet and shouting,
'Mr. Diver, I'll thank you to keep your attentions, sir, to
yourself.' And, 'Now look here, Diver, enough's enough!'
And then I was leaning back with a smile of cold amusement, 'Sufficient unto the day, my good Diver, is the
evil . . .' Then, with abrupt vigor, a boldness that caught
my breath, I saw myself take the tablecloth in hand and
rip it off in one sweeping movement, as bravely as a man
draws a sword—and Diver's plate and the flower bowl and
the food were scattered all across the room. It was won-
derful panic, as one imagines some daring exploit on the
edge of a high cliff. Then, more calmly, I rose among the
debris and with a poise of suavity offered my arm to
Madge: 'I think, my dear, home is best.'

Out of the street of stuccoed villas, round into a road
of red-stone houses. Early roses speckled a green drive
with red. There was a dampness here. A lamp standard,
faded bluish green, rose into the branches of a wide-leafed,
tropical chestnut. I began smiling: How stupid. Forty
years on—and still daydreaming like a boy of eight.

Ridiculous. Ignore the whole affair, don't expect there's
more in it than meets the eye. And, so, suddenly again
clear and laughing at myself—which was not at all
unpleasurable or diminishing, for the present self that
laughed felt itself all the more superior—I passed through
the shade of this the second street towards home.

And I remember feeling comfortable and pleased again
as I turned into my own avenue—and felt the old satisfaction of its fine width. More of a boulevard. Here the
terrace builder had laid no formulated trowel—brown
brick campaniles towered from their beards of Virginia
creeper, slate-blue château turrets squared themselves comfortably, gothic pinnacles soared high. And over all these
dead fancies the foliage of so many trees and creepers
had thrown their softening shape: the whole was cast irrevocably as a Southern English avenue, not of these
years, but of the others—springs ago that flashed the
black lacquer of carriages, summers that breathed hot
tar breath and geranium into the shade of sunblinds,
autumns of leaf smoke and a scattered rosiness of neg-
lected fruit, winters of frost on the windowpane reflecting
the morning fire in the breakfast room, flowers hot in the
conservatory, flowers and fires in the hall, smoke-smelling
fog outside and a living moving light shed over all from
the gleaming brass-bound gasolier. Years, because they
are past, of which the best is most remembered.

But half an hour later I was in the bathroom, and again
fomenting irritated visions of what—now the hour was
at hand—I must without doubt tell Diver. I think my
bathroom must have reminded me of Madge's bathroom—
where the assault had first been committed. And the sight
now of my own very bony knees tenting from the bath

water brought a vision of Diver's muscular legs—I could
see their red well-filled strength furred with syrup-colored
hairs. I remember taking the wooden lather bowl savagely
in hand and reducing my offending bones to an impersonal
foam; then I lashed soap onto my neck, screwing my eyes
up into rewarding blackness. But a sharp chemical pain
bit into my eye, it smarted so suddenly I remember floun-
dering about stupidly, feeling small and stupid and childish in the blackness as I flung my arms out and grasped
blindly for the towel that was not there. I snatched up
the bathmat and put this coarse corner in my eye. Gradually the pain cleared and angle by angle, piece by piece,
sighted along the close corner of that bathmat I saw the
old bathroom take familiar shape. The mahogany sides
of the bath, stained white with ancient water; the great
brass taps with their flat-hanging spouts sitting up like
wide-eared hares.

  —Henry, do hurry or we'll be late.

  —It's only half past five.

  —Indeed it is. And we're due next door at six.

  —No, dear—six-thirty.

  —Six. Didn't I tell you it's been changed? Now it's six.

  —Oh. How do you know?

  —He told me yesterday.

  —What?

I thought I had misheard: but at the same time I knew
I had heard it. My stomach blenched as I turned to the
door, its keyhole seemed to speak.

  —Yes, yes, dear. We were having a chat, he dropped
in for a second, he said he thought as the weather was so
nice it would be nice to sit in the garden first. He said
we could have a little glass of something.

  —Oh.

—Well, do hurry up. Saints alive, anyone would think you wanted to be rude to Mr. Diver!

I made a sudden hurried splashing noise. Muscles in my face seemed to be bursting as I forced out as quickly as I could a grating, watery laugh:

—That's a good one, Madge—whatever next! Look— I won't be a jiffy!

And I began splashing again—though this time in earnest scrubbing myself, as if Madge could see through the door.

—That's a *good* boy.

Her steps bounced away on the carpet outside. I threw the scrubbing brush away, scrambled upright, and began drying myself in haste. At all costs I had to hurry, at all costs refute this suggestion that I cared about Diver.

So she had been entertaining him? Alone in the house? She thought that by admitting this so casually she would put me off the scent? And more, even—and this was much worse—she was trying to allay my suspicions by taunting me openly with them? I hurried into my bathrobe, still wet behind the knees and about my back. They were ridiculing me? Together?

At ten minutes past six we marched down the five checker-tiled steps into the short gravel drive. Madge walked a pace in front. She had changed into a dress with short sleeves, and now walked energetically, with that brawny movement women have for the first moments of a different dress, moments it seems of challenge, when they have done everything possible with the mirror and now set out to meet, but not without anxiety, the faces of other people. They thump with their feet as they walk, they bow in their shoulders to examine for the last time the sanctity of the bosom. As for me, I was no better. I had been ready early, and I remember whistling to beat the band. But it was mostly Madge, with a last-second flurry in the larder and a slamming of the last window, who pitched a final anxiety into the last minutes. And such anxiety I translated instantly into an impatience to be with Diver; I redoubled my dark whistling.

Down the drive we walked, out through the garden-blue gateposts, onto the pavement between the two houses. From there, for the space of a few yards before we turned into the adjoining drive, the two houses could be viewed in their character as relatives: or as the one entity they assumed for the first time in my mind. Our own house—heavily ornamented, with its spired roof, its fall of newly nibbling Virginia creeper, its intricacy of Venetian blind and carriage lamp and rusted bell pull. And the other—separated only by the two side wells, a large bare white square house. It had regular black windows and a face as white as death. It had a bare flagstaff in the center of its graveled drive, it looked salt-washed and empty, like a house by the sea. But it was full of people; we saw the row of bells and names by the door as we mounted the mineral-white steps.

But already a voice was calling from somewhere; we looked down and saw Diver's head sideways coming out from the top of a sash window. A hand pointed like a fin to the corner of the house:

—Saw you coming! Round the corner, me own front door. Down and round and in.

The face disappeared. I looked quickly at Madge and saw her blue eyes open wide with surprise. Then we went down and round, round by the dustbins, and met Diver at a side door painted sudden orange. I remember it very plainly—three red-capped dwarfs nestled by the step staring it seemed in anger at a row of empty milk bottles. Diver was roaring and laughing:

—Welcome, strangers! Come into my parlor, as a well-known spider said.

Madge rang out a sudden peal of high laughter—I could not help staring at her, it came so suddenly. It was as if a row of metal bells, verdigrised but game, had suddenly become galvanized behind her nose. And in the same moment she tossed her head back, pointed a shoulder at Diver, and set her mouth wide in a great frozen smile that exposed every tooth. All she said was:

—Good *evening*, Mr. Diver.

I think I exploded my whistling into a sort of gun-shot cough. My teeth, also bared in a smile, must have looked more like burying themselves in Diver's neck. And both of us, of course, had come prepared with an opening pleasantry. So that we all began to talk at once, Madge declaring how *Bohemian* it all was, myself mumbling something about 'a nice little place you've got,' and Diver backing away in false deprecation. A dreadful moment of words and dwarfs and Madge's powder blowing as we went stumbling through the door into a dark passage that smelled of fungus.

In the dark we stood. Madge must have seen a door handle for she cried delightedly:

—Here?

But a broom fell from behind the door—it must have been a cupboard—and Diver floundered forward and caught hold of her arm. This I saw plainly. Only for a second, but the dark instantly seemed to clear. Then he had gone on and thrown open the door to a large light room full of bright colors.

Madge seemed to throw herself inside, she was applying as usual the pistons of 'cheeriness.' Already she was flitting from one object to another, praising, laughing, making the noise of horrified delight. I had followed, burning with indignation at that touch of the arm in the passage. I found myself, I remember, standing by a mantelpiece, staring alone into the mournful eyes of a long-faced Aberdeen terrier made of some plastic-like dark pumice stone. Along from this dog, I soon saw, were other glass dogs. And finally, past a celluloid calendar, there rose a large blind retriever drowned from ears to paws in gold paint. It was like the hound belonging to some sporting river god. Suddenly close behind me Diver's voice came:

–I'm very fond of dogs.

And without pausing his hand came out and thrust behind the retriever's back. Something clicked—and two bulbs in the dog's eyes flared into orange life.

It startled me, I stepped back with a jerk, felt a fool and coughed.

Madge shrieked:

–Hey, presto!

Diver roared close to my ear:

–Not bad, eh?

I felt very confused—especially in such a room. It was at first difficult to take in. There seemed no end to the sudden and startling confections that in the yellowing evening light decorated the place. The walls were distempered a fierce electric pink—and all original moldings and friezes had been picked out freshly with green, orange and silver paint; thus also the light switches, door handles, and a circular plaster flowering in the ceiling center, whose petals glowed matily like colored felt. From this central piece there depended a large black-framed ship

lantern windowed with gum-colored parchment. Against
such a heterogeny, against curtains of emerald silk shot
with pale blue jazz patterns, against an apple-green sofa,
against the glaze of a spindly table and several chairs
of machined wood that shone like brown celluloid—there
was sprinkled an assortment of dazzling objects. Orange
cushions tasseled in black; a bowl of paper tulips; a
vellum-bound book open and full of cigarettes; the cutout
figure of a parrot hanging by the window; a thin floor
vase spearing up shell-colored and pale orange dead flowers; a gramophone cabinet painted silver and green; on
a side table more dogs, and a green naked girl holding
an ash tray; ash trays glowing metallic reds and bronzes
were everywhere: and on the walls several frames, each
containing a brownish representation of medieval lettering, verses about beer; one pale blue painting of a fighter
airplane; no books, but a pile of motoring magazines.

And much more that no one could digest in those first
few seconds. Diver was saying of the walls:

–Mrs. Lawlor—that's the landlady, the dragon we call
her—let me have the place done up. A lad from the garage
did it, artistic sort of chap. I do like a bit of color about
the place. The rest of the stuff's mine—except the furniture—odd things I picked up here and there. Look at this
—cute?

He brandished close to my face a silver model howitzer
that instantly burst into long, yellow, dangerous flame.

–Cigarette lighter!

I took a step backwards, confused by the sudden flash—
now was the fellow trying to make a fool of me?—and
caught myself against the table laid for supper. Instantly
a pot of flowers in the center toppled over on its side. I
looked with horror at the strewn flowers, blushing. But

the ginger mustache just bellowed with laughter, the red meat of a huge hand reached for the flowers—and as it grasped them I saw more clearly that they were flowers made of celluloid. Diver laughed, slapping me on the shoulder.

—Insured against all risks!

Madge too rang out her strident bells—it seemed instantly that not only had Diver made a fool of me, but had contrived to patronize me at the same time, drawing Madge onto his side; the two of them were banded against me. So that now as Diver led the way out through glass doors to a veranda, my anger grew again to be righteous. I had difficulty in containing it. But I did—for there was still a doubt that possibly all this was innocent, or that in any case if I objected Diver could assume such innocence—and so I would be further confused. So retaining a shell of composure, I followed the others out through the doors.

There we found ourselves in a sort of patio, a paved yard of small dimensions walled on two sides with concrete and on the third by the wall of my own garden. It was a yard cut specially from the rest of the garden for this ground-level flat. Now it contrived a mixed appearance of Mediterranean courtyard, derelict garage, and pixie glen. We sat down carefully on chairs made from trellised branches and nailed bark; and opposite was a wall washed with sea-blue paint, where Venus revealed her stump in a sun-orange alcove: to one side lay the chassis of a motorcar, a dead-looking trestle, black tufts of oil rags and used emery paper; and this place was also the playground of more dwarfs, several colored ducks, a dovecote, and a tall stone stork.

Madge put her head so far on one side it seemed she was trying to view the scene upside down.

—Isn't it *too* pretty for words! I've often wondered from the upstairs window . . . but I never *knew*. Isn't that a sweet duck, Henry—that one in the bonnet? And did you do all this yourself, Mister Diver?

Diver pressed his chin into his neck, frowning modestly. He coughed and sucked in his teeth.

—The wall was there, they'd painted it nice and bright, and the good lady with one arm seems to go with the place. That stork too.

Then he smiled broadly, looking straight at Madge:

—But they're my dwarfs. My dwarfs and et ceteras.

I made a desperate attempt to voice my composure:

—Nice little sundial that, Diver. Interesting things, sundials. If I'm not mistaken, there's a dial on the façade of a palace in—Where was it, somewhere in Italy, Florence if I'm not mistaken . . . ?

But I was mistaken. I murmured to myself, clicking my tongue. I could never remember facts. The others waited in awkward silence. Then Diver turned away to the glasses ranged on the rustic table behind:

—Now, what'll we have?

Madge said instantly, brightly:

—What have you got?

I felt myself recede into a small corner, rejected, passed over by these conspiratory two, and at the same time infuriated with my own incompetence. I shook myself and said very loudly:

—They're accurate as clocks.

But this passed unnoticed, for now Madge and Diver were both looking hard at the glasses decorated with painted cockerels and a jug of some pale yellow liquid that Diver was stirring with a tablespoon. He was saying:

—Cup. Mixed it myself, hope it won't be too strong for you.

He poured out a glass for Madge and then at last turned to me and said:

—Cup?

I managed:

—Cup! I haven't had cup for months.

Madge said:

—No cup since Christmas.

That liquid in the fragile coned glasses tasted pale; far beneath whispered a faint and watered sickliness of gin. Madge put her glass down with a high laugh, a scale of green mint sticking to her lip like half a mustache:

—Ripping cup!

But in the meantime Diver had conjured from somewhere on the floor two short thick black bottles labeled in rich red and black scrolling with the name of a strong beer. He muttered:

—Always fancy wallop myself.

He blew out his cheeks as under some weighty duress: then poured both bottles into a large tankard, round which he cupped his great mauve hand as if it were the very staff of life. He drank—and whistled through his back teeth a jetted, belly-blown sigh.

We conversed. Madge sat in the center, so that most of the time her head was turned to Diver. It seemed that once again I was excluded. Diver refilled our glasses— and once filled Madge's without filling mine. It might have been a most ordinary oversight—Madge was explaining how to make a fig pudding—but I could not help feeling affronted.

They talked of food and shops, of Diver's new garage,

of the district's decline yet its profitable increment of
flats, of how they liked some films and disliked others,
of the necessity at all costs of keeping cheerful. Diver
said:

—You don't want to bother your head too much about
things.

—We *all* think too much.

I am normally impatient of these last remarks. I believe
industry and application to be high human attributes.
I have an almost fierce approval of knowledge. So that
now at last I raised my voice; yet I was even then muddled
about how exactly to speak my thoughts. I must have
said:

—If nobody worried about thinking things out, we
wouldn't get anywhere.

Madge laughed:

—Still, we don't want to bother *our* heads too much,
do we? Leave it to them as likes, says I.

And Diver said weightily, furrowing his huge brow:

—I'd say that history shows that people do think too
much. If it wasn't for people thinking, we wouldn't be
where we are now. What good's it all done? Unemploy-
ment, factories, smoke, and now atom bombs. . . .

His eyes took on a strange gleam, he put his head on
one side and said then wistfully from under his antlering
mustache:

—In the Middle Ages you could have a little house with
thatch on it, nobody bothering you, no rush. That's where
we'd all be, if people hadn't always worried about this
and that and thought and thought for new things.

I looked away quickly, and found myself staring at
that stone stork. Wildly I searched for argument. This
was wrong, I knew—but always such very simplification

stole my mind from myself. How to begin against such stuff? How even to remember the data to begin with? Data! All written down somewhere, all read, none remembered! Population increases? Endemic curiosity of man? Reasoning faculties? The wheel—man thought of the wheel? And then, ever recurrent—hospitals, lavatories, hospitals, lavatories . . . I said lamely:

—Well, of course that's a big question. We've got to take single instances. Take for instance . . . take *hospitals*. . . .

Complete silence. Madge and Diver were both staring at me, both holding themselves in wait. It was, abruptly, a moment of consideration, of respect. They had stopped drinking. The silence lengthened. I remember it growing, in length and in weight, so that a vast vacuum seemed to be forming, something airless and vapid, empty and dry and dull, inactive, uninspired, with myself at the root of it deflating what had hitherto been at least a dynamic collision of three people. I coughed, crossed and uncrossed my legs, beating my brain for an answer. With appalling precision my brain had become what felt like a blank forehead bone. At length I said:

—Now we wouldn't have hospitals without people in the first place thinking towards hospitals, the idea of hospitals. Now, how in the first place were hospitals conceived?

Again I paused. I did not know.

Then salvation came—a single raindrop, a fat raindrop, a plash of a drop thwacked itself like a bird drop on Madge's bare arm:

—Ooooh! Rain!

Diver jumped up and stretched his hand firmly out into the element. I, still seated, did the same. We all looked up earnestly at the sky. We waited in breathless silence.

Across the calm and falsely southern sky there had swept, as if straight from an outraged north, a pale hurrying film of cloud, it came watery white across the whole sky so that the sun shone through it, fluorescent through a film of wet wool gauze. May was gone, it was suddenly a day in February. And then, with the color of everything dulled, three or four more heavy splashes fell separate and irregular, peas lobbed from just over the wall. Then nothing. But a second later, as if these drops had been sent forward in warning, there came racing over the white a great mass of indigo, it came welling on a high wind, expanding, keeping its rounded shape, the light outlining each rounded tooth fierce silver—and then suddenly the air was deafened with a sharp, vicious, wood-splitting crack of thunder, two infinite boards of ebony slammed together. Then the rain, growling up its force like a crowd of whisperers.

Little noises of surprise and disappointment; we all rose and grabbed quickly at our glasses, at Madge's bag, at the table and chairs. Diver kept apologizing and we closed the glass doors on what was already a concreted pool of water. With relief we shut that weather out—it was like coming in from a walk on a seaside promenade. Now inside Madge and Diver laughed, breathing excitedly from their effort:

—Anyhow, it's rung the gong for supper!

Madge piped:

—Nice weather for ducks!

I stood not knowing whether or where to sit and so turned again to the windows. I think I probably said:

—This is what the farmer needs. Fine for the crops.

Then we sat down to table—each to a small green plate

of sardines and chopped carrot—and Diver with a flourish switched on the retriever's eyes. Beaming from that
darker end of the room, they glazed our plates with a
glint of premature evening. Diver gave Madge a wide grin:
   —Soft lights and sweet music!

   And as if in afterthought, but with pointed vivacity,
he turned his face at me and screwed up one side of it
so firmly that the eye vanished in a lava of purple wrinkles
and one ginger taper of mustache switched acutely up as
if to shield it. It stayed so—and I remember wondering
for a startled moment whether it was no wink but a real
seizure. However, it was a wink—intended to include me
in the joke; but instead it only convinced me that he had
grown so cocksure of himself as to throw me what seemed
a wink of consolation.

   The idea of this wink grew on me during supper: during dreadful head-bowed minutes when my plate became
a prison, when I tried to be pleasant but failed absolutely
—smiling, I suppose, with the smile of a man learning to
swim, smiling and sinking. Then other things began to
happen.

   The sardines were followed by two gravied sausages
and their mildew of pale mash; and soon after my plate
began to wobble.

   I remember glancing for one guilt-scared moment
towards my glass. The cup had been replaced by a pale
yellow beer—lighter than the nut-red brew that Diver
retained as, it seemed, some very personal medicine. At
the same time as the plate wobbled, Diver bellowed:
   —More beer, Mr. Bishop—going strong?

   I murmured my 'no'—and then once again the plate
seemed to give a lurch. Swiftly in that familiar space
where my eyes were anyway fixed I measured the move-

ment against the pepper pot, the motionless bakelite salt
cellar. Neither moved, it was only my plate. In some panic
I knew then that something lay underneath, an insect,
and a large insect at that. Cockroaches. Instantly I remembered that we were in the basement—where for dec-
ades there had been kitchens—and thought also of Diver's
bachelor state and the chances of slovenly housekeeping.
I was convinced. Awkwardly, horrified, I compromised
with the moment and began, in spite of the plate's sporadic
movement, to carve the dark-fried knob off the end of
my first sausage. I splashed this with yellow mustard,
the plate lurched, this dark wart of sausage became im-
mersed all over in yellow. At the same time I realized that
for some while the others had not been talking, I felt the
silence in retrospect, I felt that I was being watched.
Regardless of the hot mustard, I popped the sausage into
my mouth, the mustard burnt, I choked and stuffed a
paper napkin up against my mouth—and simultaneously
Madge and Diver burst out laughing. I looked up—they
were both laughing unreservedly at some object Diver
held in his hand. It seemed to be a rubber ball, attached
to a thin black tube. Now Diver squeezed the ball hard—
and my plate gave a convulsive leap. It was one of those
practical joke machines—rigged up by Diver, evidently
with Madge's collusion. I managed to laugh—a painful mustard-stained laugh. As supper proceeded Diver
brought out several more of these machines, and directed
them as much against Madge as me. The fly on the sugar,
the glass that tilts without pouring, the fork with the
electric shock. All these were produced—he was obviously
an addict. By the end I was thoroughly confused. Whenever a joke was pointed at me, I felt they were making

a fool of me. But equally, when Madge was the victim, then it seemed a further advance towards her.

Outside those windows the storm light shone bright. To hide my confusion I kept turning to look at it. Every green leaf shone brightly, poisonously phosphorescent against the dark pall above. Somewhere to the east there must have been left a patch of blue sky, for a gray-slate roof in the distance had turned bright sky-blue itself. I remember it was just when I was looking at this blue that Diver said:

—It's so easy, don't you think, to live next door to somebody in London for years and never speak to them? Seen it happen hundreds of times. It seems we're lucky enough to be the exception, eh? Exception that proves the rule?

I turned round and he was leaning forward. His mustache was somehow raised above his upper lip, so that a surprising rim of naked flesh showed between lip and mustache—was it lip, was it gum?—in what was intended as an arch confidential smile:

—I say, how about calling me Charley?

He was looking at Madge, not at me. And now this man leaned back again in his chair, looked down at his sleeve, and said in a gruff and genial voice of reason:

—I mean, all this Mister this and Mister that doesn't go far, does it?

Madge was already pealing out a lower sort of laughter, liquid and friendly. She said:

—Okay by me! Charley it is. But on one condition. You've got to call me Madge. An eye for an eye, you know.

And then, after a pause, she added:

—And Mr. Bishop's name, of course, is Henry.

I just wetted my lips with the yellow beer, and returned instantly to the safety of the plate. So a friendship had been established! No one knew to what extremes of popping in and popping out, of teas and suppers and five-minute chats, this new state would lead. All possibilities of escape were declining. I said to myself: 'Now or never —I must speak, as soon as possible, immediately after supper.' And thus I was making up my mind for the second time when Diver said something further that finally, with now no more question, decided me on the only course of direct action.

He was lolling back in his chair, secreting some strange juice of impartiality—something that gave blank distance to his eyes, that wobbled his mustache tenderly, that brought an outward thrust to his jaw as if he were apologizing for stating opinions too great for him:

—*I* like a woman to be a pal, someone you can speak your mind to, take a drink with like a man. Mind you, I don't mean *masculine* women. But look at it this way, women have fought for their emancipation, they've got it—so why shouldn't they live like men? Not that I don't put women on a pedestal—but I like 'em to be cheery. Real companionship—that's something. . . .

He stopped speaking altogether, and just wagged his head slowly from side to side. Then with a sharp effort he jolted himself out of it, smiled modestly at Madge, shook his head sharply as if rebuking himself for being a 'sentimental fool.' It seemed a direct assault upon Madge. Yet she never seemed to notice. I fumed down at four cherries and a junket floating in some kind of sticky water.

At length we rose. The thunder had come nearer, so near now that it seemed the laths of the ceiling itself

were being ripped like paper screens. I heard Madge give
a little scream. I was staring hard into that picture of a
blue fighter airplane, resentment roaring black. But in
the reflection of the picture's glass I saw Diver move over
to Madge—ostensibly to comfort her. I jerked my head
round, suddenly decided. In a strong voice—I remember
hearing it in my own ears as some separate sound, as
though my own voice were broadcasting at me—I called:

—I say, Diver—here a moment!

Diver paused, then smiled. Gratified, he smiled and said:

—Now, now. None of that Diver stuff—Charley, you
know.

I took a deep breath, raised my face to look him
straight in the eye and quickly began to speak:

—Now look here, Diver. As man to man. I've no doubt
you're a good fellow and all that, but . . .

—Well, that's decent of you, Henry.

—What?

—Decent of you to say it. I mean I like a man to say
what he thinks—

—I don't like giving advice, though I don't mind taking it. . . .

—I know, I know, Henry. No need to beat about the
bush. Charles Suffolk Diver's always ready to make allow-
ances where due. You want me to give you the low-down
on the sprightly piece of uplift to our left?

—Uplift? I don't . . .

—His Majesty's fighting aircraft as depicted in the
masterpiece to our left. I know we might not all be *au fait*
with the newfangled flying machine. Now take the wing
tips, by these you can recognize at a glance, old boy,
at a *glance* . . .

And then as Diver went on to explain the technicalities

of that sky-blue airplane, I could do nothing but swallow my silence. Diver talked so quickly. When our eyes had met it had been difficult enough to maintain the courage to accuse, now this misunderstanding had sucked all the force from me. In a way it was a relief. For a while all the breath was out of me. The parts of the airplane flew about my ears, Diver gabbled on—but then it occurred that perhaps all this was intended, it was just Diver's glib way of avoiding the situation? The blood again mounted. I turned for a second and glared at Madge, who was standing in the middle of the room holding her ears and looking fearfully at the window, as though the glass were itself a sheet of electricity.

I gave Diver a sharp tap on the arm.

—That's enough, now, that's enough—

—Get the hang, eh?

—No, look here, what I want to say is this—

—Yes, old boy, any questions thankfully received, the great Data will . . .

—About my wife, I don't think you realize—

And just at that moment Madge's hair shone gold and glinting in the glass all over the blue airplane—it was like some baleful sunrise above the clouds—then her real face was suddenly in between our shoulders, as if deliberately parting us. The lightning flashed again mauvely throwing into intense brilliance every feature—the startling chemical red on her lip, powder caked at the nostrils, bluish large pores that at times, and especially then in the lightning, gave her chin a look of lilac muscle.

—Oh, there it is again. I knew it! Count one for each mile, it's getting nearer, or is it the other way round, count towards the thunder? I don't know. Should the window be open or shut? Open the window! Won't that

let it in? Now I must take a deep breath and forget *all*
about it. Hoooh! There it goes again!

Diver had at last turned away from the picture and
was hunching himself red with laughter:

—Come, come, Madge! Worse things in the world than
thunder! How'd you like to be turned into a pillar of salt?
Nine stone of lovely Cerebos like Mrs. Lot? Standing
there all virgin white—

He seemed to have become abruptly drunk, he had
begun to wave extended fingers in front of his eyes—
fingers of the bogy man—trying through his laughter to
horrify Madge. But at the word virgin he stopped, fingers
frozen stiff in front of his eyes.

Madge herself looked startled. Then Diver wheezed in
awe:

—Strike me pink!

And then wheezed again into huge laughter, holding
his hand to his brow.

—*Strike me*—there we are back at the lightning! Nuff
said! Come on, Madge, Henry old boy. Next item on the
prog! A glass of port all round! Nout like booze to drown
the blues. I am a poet, though I don't know it!

Singing the last words, he was already over at the
table and grasping a dark bottle labeled VINTREX before
I had time to interrupt, indeed to shout now sternly:

—I say, Diver!

And this indeed must have been said with such force
that Diver suddenly stopped, bottle in one hand and
stopper in the other, his mustache at a curious oblique
slant as his nose screwed up in question and his eyes set
in a blind, perhaps even irritated, but certainly surprised,
stare.

But Madge already had the words bubbling at her

mouth, and some of them came out, nothing could stop them.

—Oh, Charley Diver, you are the limit! I don't know what you're saying half the time, I really don't. And a glass of port, how lovely . . .

Then she too stopped, seeing there was something cold and rigid between us.

I felt at last in command of the situation. He had gone far enough, now far too far with that word virgin. I was angry and exasperated. And what I had to say Madge could hear too, for all I cared. I remember standing with feet together, my arms to my sides, in a dignified attitude of attention, and I raised my chin to say loudly, emphatically:

—I repeat, man, I've had about enough of this. I've taken about as much as I can stand. Madge—

I had just turned an eye of command on my wife, when suddenly the door opened, and the face of a young woman poked itself round. She was baring her teeth and looking archly up at the ceiling. A voice, excited and tilted to one side, said shrilly:

—Any room for little me?

Without waiting for an answer, she had flung the door open and smiling at Diver was walking forward suddenly quite naturally. But behind her two other voices were looming from the passage into the faces of two young men in flannels:

—Two more candidates, a gentleman and a player!

I stood there stupefied. The whole situation had taken such a reverse—I remember not knowing at all what to do, simply standing there unmoved, I suppose like a dummy, and thus seeing more clearly what seemed more like a phenomenon than people.

Those two young men—one pink and square and the other pale, dark and large-boned, but both athletic and moving warily, awkwardly calling for more space to whirl arms and brace legs—those two young men now crowded forward and stopped fast a few feet within the doorway. They carried two or three beer bottles under each arm, they hunched their shoulders like shy gorillas. Other beer bottles stuck from the pockets of jackets stretched into distorted angles. They stood still with open mouths smiling—smiling at each other, at Diver, at the walls, the floor, at Madge and myself even. They seemed to be saying: Here we are, we two, isn't it funny, isn't it the biggest joke of all that *we two are here.*

Meanwhile Diver had been greeting the girl, calling her Norma, and this girl had been smiling up at him with the blind attachment glasses seem to give. But Diver looked straight over her head at the young men and already he was shouting:

—Dicky and Richard, the two worst men in London! And you've got the wallop?

Which I think left them nothing to say; they must have been wanting to introduce their bottles. They just stood there still. While the girl Norma whose face had stopped smiling now smiled again at Madge. For a moment nobody said anything. I could see Diver trying to hide the bottle of port held down behind his sleeve. Madge looked smiling at Norma, two women bound on expressing at least peace at first. As for me—I still stood ridiculously at attention, my words stopped, my exasperation freewheeling as these intruders accumulated.

Then once more in the twilit brilliance, in that room where only the one golden dog's eyes glared their shaded electric sin, the thunder came cracking loud and dangerous onto the ceiling. Instantly all eyes went upwards, outwards through the window, at the electric dog—and grimaces, screams, grunts of wonder were all mixed with movements forward towards each other and Diver at the top of his voice shouting introductions. Mrs. Bishop this is Dicky Carter, Richard you know Norma, Norma this is Mr. Bishop, Richard Dawk Mrs. Bishop, Norma Madge, Madge Dicky, Henry Dicky Richard, Norma Madge—so that for moments two were joined and then as suddenly unjoined and rejoined until nobody knew who was joined to whom. So they all burst out laughing.

Except myself—suddenly in the commotion I found myself extending a hand and saying 'Bishop' to Diver himself. Diver leaned hastily across to me and whispered in my ear, spitting the words urgently:

–It's all right, old man, if you've had enough just lay off it for a bit. Have another glass in a minute or two— but keep mum, old boy, breaks up the party if you don't. WHY, MRS. LAWLOR!

Most faces turned to the door again, and Diver was away and over towards a pale, elderly woman leaning slightly forward, half in and half out of the room, her hand in apology still on the doorknob.

–Am I intruding? I shouldn't really have come at all.

–SAY NO MORE! MRS. LAWLOR—COME RIGHT ALONG IN. How's YOUR BACK?

At the word BACK this lady's small, pursed lips sank tenderly inwards, her pale eyes in their dark hollows grew clouded—she seemed about to weep, sadly, endearingly. Had she lost her back a long time, many years ago? No. She straightened it bravely and coming forward with dark mauve dress drifting, with chalk-white face and dyed black hair, flashed then a bright glance of endurance directly between Diver's eyes:

—Now we mustn't mind about my back. This is a party! What fun you're all having! I shan't stay for very long.

—Nonsense, Mrs. Lawlor. You just come in and make yourself nice and comfortable. You know everyone—except Mr. Bishop over there and Mrs. Bishop talking to Mr. Dawk. But of course you must know them! Neighbors, eh? Now you come and have a glass. EVERYBODY—OUR LADY OF THE HOUSE.

With a wide gesture of ceremony he ushered Mrs. Lawlor in among everyone and then there began a clinking of glasses and a pouring from the bottles. Mrs. Lawlor, bravely smiling, had been guided to a comfortable chair and a glass of VINTREX, which Diver poured for her secretly, shielding the bottle with his huge body. I saw her catch Madge's eye for a moment, and both ladies nodded, sweetly but coldly; they were neighbors but no more than that. From then on it seemed that everyone talked and laughed and drank at once, so that the thunder itself seemed to recede, and the lightning was blanched by the livelier flickering of glasses and all those lights that Diver now switched on.

By this time I had retired from my central position to a place near the silver-painted gramophone cabinet, and now stood pressed awkwardly between the cabinet and the mantelshelf lined with dogs. The pink young man called Dicky was telling me the day's cricketing scores. He had inquired whether I 'followed' cricket; and distracted, I had nodded. Now as the score mounted and the bowlers wilted I still nodded. But I heard hardly a word. And of these people round me I saw scarcely a detail. I was unused to such a pace. But I had already retired from my

attack—a sense of propriety, and a timidity which I
remember explaining to myself as propriety, had made
it impossible for me to continue. I was fallen back, frustrated. But the frustration no longer burned; it was cooling and hardening. I held my glass of beer more firmly—
and remembered how by my first firm words I had unseated
Diver. It was obvious he had later pounced on my mistaken handshake with relief, the idea that I was a little
drunk came as a heaven-sent excuse. I knew I had wielded
a certain power. It could be resumed—this time at leisure.
And as more coldly I began to lay certain plans, the hopeless feeling of indignation left me, I was able to raise my
head, to look about, to see something of the people in some
parts of the room, to hear what was being said. Yet the
room never grew quite clear—with so many words and
so much smoke and so much movement it seemed to be
obscured by something like a cloud of flies, by some im-
perceptibly thickening and thinning dark cloud. And it
was still filling—more people seemed to have arrived, as
though put there, without ever having entered the door.
The room was swelling too big for the door, the door
once important had grown nondescript.

The muster of faces began to loll and turn like buoys
on a wave of cloth and body. Only gradually did new
faces assume names and identity. The face of a bald-
headed man with a sore-looking mustache came to belong
to 'L. H. Bradford,' not Mr. Bradford nor any prenamed
Bradford, but L. H. Bradford: it turned out he was a
writer of detective stories. There were two sharp-boned
men with tousled hair and bright wool ties who talked
strictly together, laughing only at private jokes: they
had no names. Several young and middle-aged men and
women seemed—almost startlingly—to be quite normal,

to have neither names nor identity: it was impossible to know exactly how many of these there were.

Words whirled everywhere.

—If they'd put P. B. Townsend at cover instead of R. J. B. Watts, Hudson would never have got F. C. Smith c. and b.


—Another glass, Mrs. Lawlor! My, you're looking well, I declare it does you good.

—Good? Mr. Diver, I'm not well. That seems too much to ask of life. *What* pretty flowers you have! Like shells, I always say.


—Navy's *her* color. Navy and plum.

—Of course it is. I said, I said Miss Armitage I really don't know what you mean I said. Cerise! I said.


—Good beer this, Richard, no doubt about it, good beer.

—Talking of beer, once I was down in Sussex. For Easter. Walking. Went into a little pub—just on the way as it were, not thinking at all, not dreaming of a thing at all, you know, and do you know they gave me a glass of beer that—well that was *beer*.

—I'm a Watson man. Watson and Trowley's best.


—I had him stabbed. With an icicle. Blood, wound, but no trace of a weapon. Had the deuce of a business getting rid of the footsteps, though. Meant another fall of snow.


—Now I really must go.

—One for the stairs, Mrs. Lawlor?

—Well, if she can't get plum then *wine*. And navy of course.

—Oh dear, what fun! Henry, I've been trying to get near you for minutes. Henry, was there anything wrong? Just now?

Madge. In the softer light she looked smooth and pretty, her cheeks were warm and flushed and her blue eyes I remember alive and expressionful. I saw her with affection and sudden longing, not as before like a memory but now as a loved body. But at the same time—and I have found since it is so possible to feel two opposite emotions at the same time—I remained hard, my compassion was hard, I could feel a bitter fury. But I contained it:

—Wrong? When . . . ?

—Don't be silly—before they all came. You stood up in a funny way.

—Oh, I had a bit of a turn. Must have been the thunder. Close it felt.

—Are you sure . . .

—I'm quite all right now, don't worry. Fit as a fiddle.

—Well, if you say so— Oh, there's Charley, he's got something for me . . .

Without another word her face was turned away and she was making herself thin to get through the crowd to where Charley was standing, tall and purple-faced, puffed and gleaming, winking and beckoning with his finger like a little worm. He was standing by the door.

Then Madge and he left the room together.

For a moment I stood looking at the door, amazed. A voice was speaking beside my ear:

—Aren't you Mr. Bishop that lives next door? A most

interesting drive-in you have, dark underneaths to the bushes. I was using one just the other day to hide a baby . . .

—So J. F. B. was l. b. w.!

I got to the door, wormed myself round the girl with the spectacles—she was looking through these at the door, as if in anger at Diver's exit—and then I was in the passage. A room at the end showed a light. The door was just ajar. Faint talking came muffled through the crack of light. The light was dim and pink. I stopped blundering—and very quietly tiptoed towards it. Suddenly Madge's laugh tinned out clearly.

I stood listening, holding my breath so that my ears drummed and really I could hear less than usual. But no words came through, only a muffled consonance of male and female whispering. I flung open the door.

Madge and Charley were standing by a dressing table. It was a bedroom, pink-shaded, with a divan bed. A jacket was hung on one chair, a pair of trousers lay across the bed. They stood absolutely still, their faces turned to the door wide-eyed and stuck. Charley only made one small movement, a movement of guilt, shifting his position so that his hand went further behind his back, raising a finger quickly to his tie. Then as suddenly as they had frozen they thawed. Madge laughed:

—Why, it's Henry!

—If it isn't old Henry!

I said nothing. But as Diver let out his wind of relief, he brought out from behind his back what he had been hiding, a full bottle of VINTREX, and now placed this back furtively on the dressing table.

—Thought for a moment it was that old Lawlor girl. Our noble lady of the house has already managed to get through one bottle—this is the reserve tank. Top secret, Henry old boy.

—Charley's let me into the Holy of Holies.

—Come on, Bishop, Henry. You have a drop too—it's really for the ladies, but between friends a glass won't harm. Partners in crime, eh?

—Well, I was really looking . . .

Diver came striding forward instantly. His knees bent low, he walked on his toes to suggest somehow that he was not there at all and that the whole movement was secret. He whispered at the same time at the top of his voice:

—Second door on the left, I'll show you. Put the light on, the lock's broken.

Before I could say a word, he had me out into the passage and into a small lavatory, half painted bright orange. And I was left there standing facing that orange wall and an involved nest of pipes which sprouted all over it. I waited to hear Diver go off—when the worst happened: two voices began to murmur just outside the door. They had seen the light and were wondering if the lavatory was really occupied. In a moment they might try the door! It was ridiculous, but I felt I had to wait a reasonable period. I even thought I might as well take advantage of the position. But this was impossible, my nerves were upset. Then the door opened but as quickly shut again with a coughed apology. So I just stood stiffly upright, not daring to move, staring stupidly up at a little frosted window above the pipes. Then down at the pipes, leaden twisted shapes leading in all directions. There was nothing so wrong about Madge having a drink of port? Just the sort of fellow who'd hide his drink?

Still—in the bedroom? Something unsavory, too familiar about the whole affair.

I pulled the chain hard several times, making a noise loud and grinding as possible, waited a further few seconds, and then turned and opened the door. Two young men were standing outside; they suddenly stopped talking. I tried not to look at them and went straight back to the bedroom. There was no Madge, no Charley—only Mrs. Lawlor bent searching by the bedside table. She straightened up quickly as I came in, so quickly that a pain must have caught her and she clutched quickly at her spine:

—Oh, my back! What a surprise you gave me.

—I'm so sorry. I thought . . .

—I was just looking for—I thought perhaps my bag— but really it doesn't seem—now where have I seen you before?

In her mauve draperies Mrs. Lawlor swayed as she peered forward. She was drunk. But in those few seconds she had nevertheless contrived to hide her search, recognize me, make her excuse and then forget who I was— lapsing into a pause between each action as completely void and purposeless as the texture of her eyes, now so dull beneath their hooding lids. She peered forward at me, a slight convulsion traveling past the locket on her swathed chest. She came forward slowly, stiffly:

—Oh, you do remind me of someone, someone *I know very well.* . . .

I stuttered some sort of apology and left her still advancing on the wall space where I had been standing.

The party was at that same level—the noise and movement and dark upper cloud were the same. I felt as though I had never left the room, it was like a music switched off and on. Then I saw Diver was laughing with Madge over by the blue airplane. As I came in, he saw me too and barged through to ask if I had seen Mrs. Lawlor. I felt he had left Madge too abruptly to ask this question: as though he should not have been talking to her. I told him that Mrs. Lawlor was in the bedroom and he blew out his cheeks in mock terror and bolted out of the door.

Then, like a storm subsiding, the room abruptly grew quiet. The laughter echoed and sank, movement dawdled to a stance, only the smoke remained. Scattered sentences shot in and died on what was almost silence. I noticed people looking at each other as if they had never really looked before. Only the smoke hung still deeply clouding this extraordinary nonmovement. The drink had run out.

But now Diver crowded in the doorway with Mrs. Lawlor on his arm, pushing this dazed lady a little in front of him. In such a suddenly aimless room this made quite a commotion, everybody looked round. Some special sense of the opportune—highly developed in the alert faces of salesmen—told Diver exactly what was the state of affairs, so that instantly he broke into a loud and cheerful laugh:

—What? The wallop run out? There's only one thing for it, mates. A fighting retreat—into that commodious citadel known to one and all as the Claverton!

This I knew was a public house near by. Several people cheered, not least the two young men Richard and Dicky, and there was general laughter—the puritan laugh confessing enjoyment in drink. One or two bottles were collected, several moved towards the door. Dicky and Richard pretended they were running. Mrs. Lawlor remained dazedly standing by the center table, yet managing to swivel most keenly her filmed eyes round the room at a level of small tables and those low shelves upon which bottles are sometimes left. One or two of those neutrals, including a young red-haired woman in trousers whom I had never noticed at all—one or two came up to thank Diver, saying they were not going out but going 'upstairs.' Hearing this, others who were going out said: 'See you later, then.' And it seemed that in the great house lumbering high above there was to be another party. But of course it was only that several of these people lived in rooms above—it was a house of furnished rooms.

So the room was quickly empty. My wife and myself and Diver and Mrs. Lawlor were left. Diver was explaining that there would be drinks now at 'the local,' and that afterwards they might bring some beer back. Through the hanging tobacco smoke against the cushions and furniture tousled and disarranged, against the sweet reek of empty glasses and the black-stubbed dry smell of ash, against the new points of light of all the odd glasses everywhere, Diver's large brown suit and redly ginger face showed full of effort and life. He boomed:

—Now you must come along, I insist.

—Well, Charley, it's very nice of you—

—Perhaps it's not so much in your line, but nowadays it's really all right, all sorts go, pubs are different.

Then Madge, still laughing through her words, said what I had not expected.

—Well, I really think all things considered not tonight, no, really, not tonight.

—Oh, but Madge! Henry, make her come! You'll come?

—No, really.

Diver made a deep-sighing gesture and said that it was a great, great pity. He moved towards the door. At any other time I would have seen clearly that this was only a reasonable attitude for Madge to take—for after all

we were the oldest in the room, a decade older or more
than any of the others, and much more indeed in terms
of habit. Madge had seldom entered any of the neighbor-
ing public houses. I suppose we still regarded them as
vaguely improper. But then I could do no more than
construe her refusal in terms of what had occurred that
evening. I knew that Madge was refusing only so that
Diver would become more interested; she was thrusting
him back to bring him on—making sure of the future.
And this made me say:

—Are you sure, dear? Why not let's go—for once!

Diver clapped me on the back. Madge looked quickly
with surprise.

—I must say Henry seems to be enjoying himself tonight!

—I certainly am!

—But really, I don't think we can go. Not tonight.

Diver got the finality in Madge's tone. And once spoken
I scarcely wanted to press my point; I felt tired myself;
I had thrown it in more as an expression of what I thought
than as a real wish. Then we moved out into the passage
—and the girl Norma with the glasses came hurrying
back. She smiled up at Diver and in the half-dark I saw
her take his arm:

—Aren't you coming, Charley?

Diver tried to disengage his arm, though he was smiling
at her. He said with a trace of impatience:

—In a minute. Just seeing Mr. and Mrs. Bishop to the
front door.

—Oh, Mr. and Mrs. Bishop? Mr. Bishop is it, Mr. Bishop
who has the hairdresser's?

With her free hand she patted her hair, and shone those

rimless glasses at me. Diver moved us along with sudden brusqueness. He began to talk about Mrs. Lawlor:

—I really didn't know she liked her drop so much. Half an invalid, hides herself up in her room most of the time. I suppose it's all right to leave her. Her house anyhow, she'll go upstairs.

—But oughtn't you to say good night?

—Shh! Between you and me, I don't think the dear lady would understand!

Now we were out by what Diver called the front door, the back door with the dwarfs and milk bottles. Diver seemed to be acting with some impatience. He had pulled away his arm, I saw him frown and shake his head at Norma. Norma looked sad and let her shoulders suddenly slope. I guessed then that there was something between those two. And that it was plain Diver did not want Madge to see.

At the gate we all said good night.

Later, before getting into bed, I said to Madge:

—Nice people those. We ought to see more of them. Sometimes I think we keep ourselves to ourselves too much. Times are changing.

Madge looked at me curiously:

—It's not only the times. Do turn that light out.

## 3

A week and a day later, on a Sunday in the afternoon, the front door slammed. I was left alone in the house, in that sudden curtain of silence which drops on an empty house with the echo of the door. I remember standing in the hall for a moment, listening. Madge had gone out for the afternoon—her sister had telephoned, she had gone over to tea. The sister lived farther out by half an hour's bus ride. It meant that Madge would be away for a good two hours.

I made sure she had gone, then turned quickly towards the silent staircase; it was a moment I had been waiting for. I made straight for those brown-carpeted stairs but paused. An idea occurred, and I turned and moved slowly to a door opposite, the door of what I call my 'library'—what Madge calls the 'den.' I walked across to where the pale oak desk stands—and took out the key.

This was unquestionably 'my' room. I always felt safe there, I could rely on not being interrupted. That made it my 'den.' But in one sense it was a library—bookcases containing my father's scientific works covered one entire wall. Otherwise, the pale wood and a chill green paper

gave the place a severe look I liked, the severity of a
school laboratory; and in it I was surrounded by objects
of old familiarity, a glass case of pinned moths, a brass
microscope, a baize tray carrying fragments of crystal
and oölite—dull things, but of some sentiment to me, and
of a reassuring maleness that must have dated from
schooldays. No curtains, but green rolled blinds. And
momentous at one end the great gothic pale oak desk
whose front rolled back.

Inside, I cleared out three drawers. Papers, letters,
paperclips, nibs, coins—all smelling of rich pencil shav-
ings. I stuffed them up into the pigeonholes above. Three
empty drawers were left. I remember working with method
and relishing a sense of tactic. I took a duster and cleaned
each drawer carefully. Then tried the lock of each drawer.
Each worked smoothly. I took the key and attached it
to my key ring: then went to the door, opened it, and
stood for a moment listening.

Not a sound. The stillness of a Sunday afternoon, a
Sunday with a low white London sky, ragged outside with
small winds; Sunday indelible in every muffled minute.
Why? The memory of the morning church bells? The stillness without traffic? The special amplitude of midday
dinner? The knowledge of the week's accepted day of rest,
a whirring down of the works? Enid the maid out for the
day? But suddenly I lost this sense of Sunday—it became
strangely a weekday afternoon. Just such an afternoon
in a still, empty house—in this particular house where
I had spent my childhood—when sometimes after my
mother had gone out, I was left alone . . . and had crept
cautiously up to her bedroom to inspect with held breath
the many secret marvels that lay in the drawers. I was

climbing the stairs to that same room. Only now it was my wife's bedroom.

The room was deadly still, stiller than in the echoing hall—it was a female room, there were bright motionless mirrors and a clean silken look about the bedspread and pale silk curtains. Everything stood breathless clean. Everything was in its place, swept, dusted, polished, square and spread exactly, folded and placed in drawers. The satinwood surfaces shone. Silver hairbrushes mirrored themselves three times, but with astounding lack of movement, in a triptych mirror on the dressing table. Pale blue was Madge's color. After father died, this was one of the first rooms she had redecorated: with the blue went a cream wallpaper and a peach-colored carpet. Over these colors there hung a faint perfume, a pinkish-white Englishwoman's perfume of fresh flowers, a powdery smell. Dry now as the silence.

I always felt awkward in that room. Too large, too male in my dark clothes against such female tricks. I went forward and then—caught sight of someone in one of the mirrors! It came creeping stealthily in another direction —my own profile—but something bumped in my throat. I remember looking round quickly. No one was there of course, nothing but the open white door and the dark space of escape to the landing outside.

Then I began.

One drawer after another came open. I ran my hands through things quickly, taking great care to place them back exactly in their first position. I felt clever. Another man might have forgotten—but my particular business had given me a flair for such neatnesses. Sometimes I paused, handled some object with a certain surprise—a small scent spray, a case full of nailfiles, three cards onto which artificial roses were stitched. Never before had I seen these—they were possessions of my wife of which I knew nothing. What a strange, secret life a woman must live among such secrets—how many times Madge must have turned over these things, considered them, and with nothing said! How had she got them, bought them? This unfamiliarity seemed to stimulate me—I went on looking the harder. Now into the lower drawers, feeling with my hands among the silk things folded there, among stockings and soft underclothes and the hard carapace of a corset. Then—in the bottom of the bottom drawer, tucked far inside—I felt a box. I drew it out, excited. A lacquer box. Locked.

I tried it—perhaps it was jammed—and then shook it. Something rattled inside. I picked up a hairpin, bent the end, and tried the lock. But the trick was forgotten— once, a long time ago, perhaps as long ago as when I had marveled quietly in this same room when it was my mother's, I had known. But not now. It was plain the key had to be found. The lacquer box stood now on the dressing table, shining and clean and closed. The key— I went instantly to the pots on the dressing table, opened them, looked among the little things inside. In one there was the corner of an envelope. On this a telephone number had been written in pencil, a number in the same district. I took out a notebook and noted it, methodically bracketing against it: 'Silver dolphin pot on d t.'

Suddenly a door slammed downstairs. Quickly but with precision, I put back the lacquer box and piled over it the camouflage of underclothes. I closed the drawer—it had all taken a second—and went quietly out onto the landing. I listened.

A creaking came. But I felt safe on the landing, safe

away from the bedroom. Fearing Madge's return, I had
forgotten the common fear of an intruder: I went quickly
downstairs, not even bothering to keep quiet. The creaking came from the kitchen. The intersecting door stood
wide open. I went towards this—and through in the
kitchen saw a cupboard door slightly swinging. As it
swung it creaked. I stopped, startled back now to the possibilities, then crept forward, keeping in the shadow of
the wall. I paused by the door, looked through the crack
—there would be a shadow if somebody was standing behind. But it showed light through. Then I caught myself
crouching, felt stupid—the householder!—and irritated,
walked straight into the kitchen. A scullery cloth flapped
—and I saw that the back door was open. That was all.
Then I sniffed. There was a faint smell of pipe tobacco
on the air.

I caught it again—and then it was gone. I remember
walking round sniffing; but the smell was gone. Had I
ever smelt it? I was sure—yet knew my nerves were perhaps overalert, possibly the smell had been imagined?
After all—I had been thinking of a male intruder, a
tramp, a housebreaker, and this might have translated
itself into a male smell . . . however, there was something strange, something else—for a door had slammed
and this back door was open. I went over to the cupboard
door and slammed it. It closed with a rubbery quiet, air-
tight. I looked back into the hall, along the dark passage
with its watered reddish light shed by a stained window
beyond. Perhaps somebody was already in the front
rooms? I shut the back door. Then paused with my hand
on the bolt; then did not bolt it, for somehow this was
an escape route, I was not sure for whom.

I walked down the passage and went through every

room in the house. All were empty. I opened each door quickly, keeping away from it at the same time—from behind doors a man can strike. All through the resonant empty house, each room ticking quiet. But no one. I felt all the alert unease of such absolute emptiness, all the population of staring furniture. I noticed suddenly chairs and pictures that I seemed not to have seen for years. The pale Sunday light came in past the high dark shrub outside, embedding each room in water glass. I remember having the feeling that I was following myself; I felt my shadow. At length, as each room was conquered, the disturbed feeling—it was hardly fear—left me; I scarcely looked at the last few rooms. Yet through all this, beyond a half-felt unbelief that anyone would break into my house on a *Sunday* afternoon, a suspicion had arisen—supposing it had been Diver? Diver looking in, on the chance of catching Madge alone? Peering about, not daring to walk in farther? . . . Still—why not the gardener, the gardener sometimes came on Sundays? Or someone looking for Enid—the maid Enid? But I was tired by the long walk round, tired of creeping about my own house. For a moment I must have seen things quite straight and grimaced—making a fool of myself! I went back to Madge's bedroom. This time I walked in with more confidence, even sat down on the dressing-stool as the search began again.

I opened a powder bowl and found not powder but a diary and an address book. The excitement came back, I bent down carefully to examine these two treasures—what I had really come to find. All my guilt returned, I stopped to listen for the silence—then turned back the pages. I found the day Diver had first appeared in our lives.

*May 12th. Morning, silver. Miriam rang. C.D. came from next door.*

There it was—written in purple indelible pencil! The ruled lines and the dates in the diary embraced this message with a special emphasis of forbidden paper.

*May 14th. C.D. with screw driver, a lively sort.*

*(Dine Saturday 6:30 not 7.) Hair set Saturday 12.*

I was suddenly small and wretched. Why had she only noted these references to the Diver dinner? Had nothing else happened the whole day? A special hairdressing for Saturday? Why Saturday? What was the meaning of 'lively sort'? I grew angry. Putting the worst construction on it, managing both to hope I was wrong yet delight in some righteous way that I might be right.

*May 16th. Hair set 12. Gardener 3. Dined C.D. evening. Party. Nuff said.*

What was so extraordinary was that the words were actually there, written down, in that hard purple pencil. She must have sat somewhere, on the same stool I was sitting on, filled with private thoughts that had distilled themselves into these words. It was plain that the affair was important enough to write down. (Certainly there were other notes, on other days and about many other matters—but these seemed not so aware, not so *purposeful* as these three references to Diver. These were confessions.) Much secret thinking—small smiles, perhaps a sigh. My indignation rose—I could not help thinking of Madge in her underclothes silhouetted in the bathroom window.

But with a kind of nervous gluttony I went on turning the pages. But nothing had been written at all—nothing for a whole week! And this was the most important week— I certainly hoped to find a note of some meeting about which she had kept silent. But nothing at all! She had simply stopped writing the diary for a week. It was hopeless, I felt tricked and furious at this dilatory inaction, this casual laying aside of a daily task. I remember the feeling, though I scarcely admitted it then, rather discarded it to that insatiable back of the mind—the feeling that I had *hoped* for something. And with it no negative hope, no dread; it was an excitation of positive hopefulness, a positive desire for an admission of infidelity. Perhaps for something with which to torment myself, perhaps for evidence that would damn them and finally prove my suspicions.

Looking up and out through the window, past the mirror frame, past the planes in the avenue and to the roofs opposite—I saw the afternoon had grown dark. There were two houses in view, one mansarded with slate-blue and the other studded with turrets of a deep burnt red. Both roofs shone damply, a light rain had started. The clouds had crept lower, and had turned brownish-gray, heavy with water. A cold little wind shook the branches, sent a rag of smoke away at an angle and into nothing. I felt this gentle lowering, this scrappy gloom of the weather—and wondered what next to do, whether in fact anything was worth doing. Nevertheless I took out my notebook and copied carefully each of the three pertinent diary entries, noting the dates exactly. Then three or four telephone numbers—those which were written in indelible lead—discarding the others and approving myself for this cleverness. Looking round the room I saw to it that everything was in place—even touching things, arranging them elsewise, then rearranging them—and finally turned to leave. On my way to the door I saw a fold in the bedspread. This I straightened—I do not believe for my own satisfaction, but because I knew that Madge liked things exactly neat. I think I did this genuinely out of friendly habit for Madge.

On the way downstairs, the words kept muttering in my brain:

—Nuff said . . . nuff said . . . nuff said. . . .

It was a phrase my wife often used. It had two connotations—when something was to be condemned so that further mention was imprudent; and quite conversely when times were so good that more description was unnecessary. 'Good' here often implied 'naughty' or 'wicked' —the two became synonymous when applied to something approved of, as a man in his cups can be called a 'wicked old dog' if you like him or 'disgusting' if you don't. The phrase thus could mean anything. But Madge had enjoyed herself that evening—there was little doubt that this must be a positive 'nuff said.'

I went down to the library, and walked quickly over to the desk. With precision, with the satisfaction of a job well done, I placed the notebook in the drawer and locked it. I wandered away, thinking—but suddenly turned back to the desk, unlocked the drawer all over again to take out the notebook and turn up those telephone numbers. Then I rang each number and asked for Mr. Diver. The third number said he was out. And who was calling?

That voice a few inches from my ear spoke like a midget's voice from a distant toy world, repeating 'Who's there?' I held my breath, made no sound at all, awful alternatives occurring to me. 'Oh, just a friend' and 'Robert Callingham' (which was the name of a boy at school long ago, with whom I had had no real acquaintanceship, but whose name had continually occurred to me ever since). But I never dared, I just waited and as the voice spoke the third time, high pitched and like an angry dwarf—very gently I placed the receiver on its plastic trestle that clicked with a soft finality.

The next two hours I spent pacing up and down that long room, restless, sitting on various chairs. Some of them I had not used for years; I remember the room taking on dangerous new angles. Irritated, excited, confused—but from the confusion came an idea. It would have started with that telephoned voice from Number 48. On the evening of the party I had felt alone against these who were friends of Divers'. Not only because they were perhaps too young and fast and altogether of another generation and way of thinking; but in my mood of being 'left out of things' I had seen them all as being much on the opposite side of the fence. But now, thinking of them again, I saw that in fact they could be made useful. It would be difficult to become intimate with them—there were the plain differences of age and interest—but nevertheless it could be tried. If I could make them my friends, I would get to know more than by any other means. It was a possibility. At six-thirty I collected my cap and stick and went to the front door.

But outside I passed Number 48, went walking slowly down the avenue. A direct call would look obvious. But it was very likely some of them would be in the Claverton Hotel.

The Claverton was shut. The doors glassy black and closed double, an iron grill covering the saloon entrance, no sign of life or light inside. It was only twenty to seven —on a Sunday they never opened until seven. So I thought I would take a walk on down to the waterworks. I had left a note for Madge—saying in fact that I had gone for a stroll to the waterworks gardens. It was a favorite short walk, the gardens were quite peculiar—freshly green, neatly asphalted, a geometric paragon of wet green discipline. It occurred to me that it would be just as well to walk up there, take a turn by the laurels and privet; in a way it satisfied my conscience. Now I could say to myself I had written the truth.

Down the hill then by a steep side avenue to the lower ground where the pumping station stood, its acid emerald cupolas clustering low among the roofs and brown brick. It was always like descending from the hills to some fabulous citadel of the east. Byzantine in brown and white tiles, it stood behind firm gray railings. From these to the precise walls stretched the clipped lawns, the low square clumps of golden privet and green laurel—it seemed that these evergreens were suckled wet by the great wealth of water underneath, a clear liquid richness pumped up and always flowing through the engines of that so sanitary house. For a moment I sat on a seat outside the railings and looked in with approval at the absolute slate orderliness of the asphalt paths. This engine house with its sensible scientific function and the sober romance of its architecture, with its etched cleanliness— as though about it there always hung a gray light purer than the sunlight—this place always reminded me more exactly than anything else of the engravings of new architectures pictured in my father's books. About it there was no decay, here was a living remnant of the great age of scientific belief. I loved the air, the solidity, the promise.

Two white-flanneled figures came striding round the corner, they walked fast, gravely not talking, intent on their inner mechanism. Carrying tennis rackets and white cardboard boxes of tennis balls, they were those boys Rich-

ard Dawk and Dicky Carter. As they came swinging to
within a few yards I turned, swallowed my apprehension,
and smiled at them straight in the face. They slowed
down:

—It's Mr. Bishop! How *are* you?

—Didn't we meet at Charles Diver's place? How do
you do?

—Fine.

—Oh, grand.

There was a pause.

—Been playing tennis?

—Yes . . . oh, yes.

—I thought so, saw you had your bats.

—Our rackets? A few sets up in the park, singles. More
fun singles. I suppose—I suppose you're out for a walk?

—Just to the waterworks and round.

There was another pause, it was difficult. Then I said
what a good party it had been—they agreed, they had
'gone on' until after midnight. A pause. We agreed how
lucky it was that the weather had cleared, nothing worse
than a wet Sunday (if it wasn't a wet Monday). And
then they said they must be off, it was no good hanging
about in the open with a sweat on, was it?

I knew by the way Dicky the pink one had kept glancing up at the waterworks clock that he had been anxious
about seven o'clock. They were off to the Claverton. I had
purposely not suggested joining them, it would have
looked too direct—and they might have refused, hedging
away from an older man. So I waited ten minutes more
before walking up the hill again and entering the open
and warmly lit public house. I went into the saloon bar
and walked straight to the counter without looking to
either side and ordered myself a glass of beer. I remember

drinking half, gazing as though abstracted straight in front of me—at a mahogany overmantel lined with gleaming bottles and cards displaying aspirin packets—before turning, leaning an arm on the counter, to look most casually round the bar.

Richard and Dicky, white-flanneled against the dark wood dado, sat in a far corner in shadow beneath dark lusterless mirrors. They had pint tankards on the wicker table in front of them, they sprawled easily, relaxed and in health. Richard looked up then and caught my eye— he smiled, raised a finger in salute. But no move was made. Strategically by the bar, I knew that at one time or other they would come to refill their glasses; it was better to wait, not to force anything. With the beer inside me, I felt already more at ease, magnanimous rather. I could feel this magnanimity and a pitiless craft at the same time; feelings of the moment and intentions for the future do not necessarily associate. Quite at ease then, with leisure to look round this unfamiliar bar which in the future I was to know so well.

Mahogany, darkened in places to black, framed walls of cut and frosted mirror. Such mirrors bright with electric light made the place twice as lively; they must have been put in long before the turn of the century. But these, and two large black glass surfaces decorated with the curled gold announcement of an old brand of ale, crowned and medaled, and the whole heavy mahogany surround of frames and pillarings and broken pediments had not been left alone. On some of the mirrors tall green flamingos and birds of paradise had been painted at some later date, itself forgotten; a new fireplace tiled with etiolated lilies and tulips had been put in; on the original bulbous brass gasolier system at the end of the counter now hung large red silk lampshades fringed with black beads; two or three new wicker tables carried astringent green glass tops. Yet overall, despite these additions, there hung still an atmosphere of the oldest dark time, not of the tavern but of good Victorian polish, richly glassed and brassed. With the smell of old food and stale wine hanging in every corner, the place seemed mellowed in dust—but not so much household dust as the dust of cobwebs in a wine cellar.

In its way it was pleasing. But I soon found that was only its present emptiness. The quiet sanctified it as a museum piece, dressed in these obsolescent features with some nostalgic grace. But soon the doors were swinging open and people filling the place. People of contemporary appearance, dressed in colors of harshly modern brilliance or mackintoshed and muddily khaki. All character, of bar and people, became submerged.

—We meet again!

Richard was there on my left, tall in a white sweater, smiling from his deep eyes, inquisitorial small eyes under the big-boned white forehead. I was going to greet him when I saw that his eyes—thoughtful though they were—stared too far above mine. I turned and found standing behind me that L. H. Bradford, who then greeted me rather than Richard, perhaps because we were more of an age, and sealed matters by buying us both a drink and suggesting a move to the tables. So I followed Bradford's balding head and grease-stained mackintosh over to the mirrors. I was rather pleased at the success of my maneuver—but decided to let the talk run on, to keep my ears open, not to mention Diver until later.

They chatted, I said little—only nodded and laughed at the right moments, making myself as affable as I could.

From this remove an attitude so consciously calculated seems distasteful, but it must as well be borne in mind that all this had been imposed upon me in the first place by others: I was the injured: it was I who had been attacked. This was defense—my methods had to descend to the level of the aggressor. So I acted. I made my eyes twinkle at Dicky, smiled more seriously at Richard—thinking of both these adult young men in their middle twenties as children, but carefully treating them thus individually as a jolly pink fellow and a thoughtful sensitive boy. To L. H. Bradford I presented a graver face, meeting his eye with a courteous grave sympathy, sometimes deferential—deference to please the man of letters. In fact I became so intent on these calculated mannerisms that the meaning of the conversation began to pass over my head. Only half through some saying of Richard's did I realize the boys were in fact discussing Bradford himself. A description that was really directed at me—but which Bradford himself seemed to be enjoying with relish.

–. . . as cold-blooded as they make them. Merciless to those that cross his path, a student of retribution. A nasty, nasty fellow, eh, Dicky?

–I should say—what about that burglar business?

–You mean my little check?

–No, the gin. Tell Mr. Bishop about the gin, L.H.

–The gin? The gin my hospitality offers the visitor of the night, the dark intruder? Well, Mr. Bishop, you know my business is crime. At a remove, let us admit—but nevertheless crime. I know a lot of the crooked classes— my material, my bread-and-butter. From their misdeeds I turn an honest penny. And thus—I say to myself—what can I do in some return? For services rendered? This is where the gin comes in. Sometimes I am away from home.

The room—a balcony room—is shut up. Sooner or later the word'll get round. I shall be visited in my absence. Naturally I'm worried . . . this is my one opportunity to offer some return to these patient donors of my bread and of my butter. I considered this—and formed a habit. So that now I never leave the house without putting out on the table a plate of cake and a bottle of gin—a full bottle. Let them, I say, enjoy themselves.

The stubbled mustache leaned back, the arrogant eyes gazed round the company with a blankness of question, their tufted brows raised for approbation. They stared at me. Something had to be said:

—Extraordinary, Mr. Bradford. A most unusual move —but I can see, in its odd way, I can see it's generous. It doesn't sound as though you're as ruthless as Mr. er— Richard believes.

Dicky then cut in, bubbling with laughter:

—But the bottle's full of . . .

Before he could finish there came again Bradford, speaking with pronounced suavity, eyes lowered to regard the grimed nails of his yellow fingers:

—Full, to be precise, of a solution of glauber salts. An odorless solution, primed with a touch of gin to smell right. Not enough to kill. But certain to create some hardly less decisive symptoms within the hour.

At which Dicky broke into laughter—in which I had to join, though inwardly with some distaste. Bradford for some seconds maintained the study of his nails. He smiled, shrugged his shoulders, looked modest.

Then he stuck some shape into his amorphous jaw, raised his eyebrows, turned his head towards the bar and with a flourish—not entirely serious but patently bred from some wish that it could be so—with a thumping flourishing hand on the table called to the bar for more drinks all round. I watched him carefully, undeceived by such affectation, but impressed by a certain initiative the man seemed to have. I leaned forward—Bradford was winking at the elderly hennaed barmaid—and said:

–But, Mr. Bradford, this kind of thing—do you actually do it?

Bradford looked at me in surprise:

–Good heavens, yes. And more like it—whenever it pays.

Richard looked up from his drink and said something which made me start—for it echoed curiously my own thoughts—not in the always rather playful tone of the others:

–Isn't that rather the question, whether it pays? At all?

–Pays? But of course it does.

–I mean it in the larger sense—does it pay to be so unscrupulous, to administer this private justice, so intolerantly, so efficiently . . . I mean does it do you yourself any good? Inside?

–Hello, Richard's up in the sky again—going, going, gone!

–Shut up, Dicky. You know what I mean, L.H. Don't you feel some dirty sensation of triumph . . . ?

–But it isn't *dirty* to win, to succeed.

–Isn't it? I should have thought you took a sort of delight in it that wasn't too pure. There's a ruthlessness about it all that suggests you don't feel at all for the loser. You've no sympathy—to win at all successfully you must sort of feel what it's like to lose. . . .

–Richard, you make me feel quite creepy. Is this a morgue or a pub? Drink up! And I'll tell you a few more of my dirty successes. . . .

I emptied my glass, glad a little that this was a pint

glass tankard, that I could lose my face in it. As often happens when the mind is preoccupied, every word spoken round, every other person's character seemed to have some relation to the problem within oneself. Richard, I could see, was a thoughtful boy—indeed quite unlike Dicky, inseparable though they seemed—and had for a moment nearly destroyed my growing belief in this eventful initiative of Bradford's. I saw for a moment—and it was not so difficult, with Bradford's decaying face straight in front of my eyes—how unhappy a man like that could make himself; I saw too clearly that something of my own attitude in the last few days might have been compared to Bradford's. But, on top of Richard's query— here was Bradford resilient, uncaring, easily putting the question on one side! It could not trouble him much. He was of course an author, this had to be considered—possibly he was different to other people? Richard and Dicky were beginning to discuss cricket scores. So I caught the opportunity to say to him:

—What was the name of your last book again, Mr. Bradford?

He looked startled, abruptly his face seemed to lose some of its life:

—Book? Mine? You're mistaken, I haven't actually . . .

—But I thought—

—Oh, that I wrote detective books? Crime fiction and all that?

—How silly of me, it must be stories in some magazine.

—In none you've ever read, Mr. Bishop. Let's be frank. Five years ago even I'd have answered your question differently. I'd have hedged, said the last book was out of print, et cetera, et cetera. But now it's too late. I've admitted it to myself too often.

He sighed. Then:

—D'you know what I do? Every week I churn out stuff for the cheapest of all the pulp you see on the cheapest of all bookstands. Not even magazines. Threepennies.

His voice stopped as he shrugged his shoulders. It was not despair, but instead a gray sort of sagging, a tiredness, a loss of faith that half drooped off the mask of indifference, yet itself so indifferent that even the strength of resignation was lacking. He was simply tired of regretting; the interest had gone.

I mumbled that I was sorry. Indeed I was—sorry to see this sudden dejection, this mild crumbling of an edifice I had thought inviolate; sorry too, in a sort of projection of myself. So I was glad when Bradford began to brighten again as he said:

—But it's no use crying over spilt milk. At least I do fairly well for myself—as a business concern. I don't really even believe that old sense of ambition is quite wasted . . . I mean it was there, and it's got to go somewhere, it isn't natural it should leave a hole. If professionally you don't succeed, you transfer into a different sphere—you must still do something with that spark in you. Me, I like to potter about with these little ideas of mine that Dicky here finds so ingenious. That and other things.

Here Bradford smirked and looked mysterious. He had quite recovered himself, he had his esteem again. I felt relieved, in fact I remember clutching so eagerly at Bradford's return to esteem that the man seemed more admirable than before. And I chose this moment to say:

—I do understand you. For some it isn't so simple. Others find their feet so easily. Now who—who could one cite . . . What about Diver? He seems a happy man,

knows what he's about. Wouldn't you call him—I know
in perhaps a small way—successful?

—Charley?

Bradford leant back and laughed.

—Charley successful?

He raised himself quite upright in his chair, looked
away to the side, as though searching for light or for air,
and made several small coughing sounds before returning
his eyes with a frown to peer closely into mine:

—Charles Diver is a paragon of ill-success. Do you know
what he would like to be? Charley would like to be standing in a Piccadilly showroom, in a sleek suit tailored in
Savile Row, on a sleek floor paved with shining tiles, sell-
ing at sleek prices the longest and sleekest limousines
through his equally long and sleek mustache. That's
Charley with a halo, that's your dream Charley. And
when the heavenly showrooms shut, haloed Charley would
be off to a small new club with a thick carpet and gleaming bottles. There would be double Scotches and earnest
racing discussions: there would be thoughtful silences as
Diver the expert delivered the last word: there would be
more double Scotches: then in a car with a huge bonnet
he would drive several streets away at great speed to
another small club with another new carpet; a club full
of models—lovely lady models. Then Diver and the chosen
lady model would go out to drink and eat and dance, talking earnestly and knowledgefully of cars and clubs and
theatrical personalities they had met, until they were
three-quarters way down the whisky bottle in some car-
petless bottle club at three or four in the morning. Inter-
mittently, haloed Charley would deliver sly glances at
other lady models seen on the way, glances that sealed
future assignations. And then he would see the lady model

home to his bed. The next day he would describe their barren little function together in delighted detail to other bag-eyed gentlemen at lunch; the episode would be called 'pleasuring her.' With luck she would be said to have been 'good value.'

My inside sank. I remember being fascinated and moved —not disgusted—at this confirmation of Diver's prowess with the ladies. I was horrified and in some perverse way pleased. I wanted more:

—How extraordinarily well you put it!

Bradford's eyes were alive and reflective; he no longer looked lost and weak, but now in some way pulled together. He took a large gulp of his beer and began again. Behind him the bar was filling; there was smoke; faces and shoulders were jostling. The mirrors reflected this and themselves grew more to life.

—That's the dream Diver. But what is he really? In the first place past his prime—not so much in years, as in wastage. He's never had much whisky, but he's run himself down on beer, beer, beer. He's grown red and flabby with beer and his showroom is a small garage in this be-nighted hole. He's never developed the taste to dress as he would—he just doesn't know, his shoes are too pointed, and his color sense is hell. He can't talk in his godlike West End drawl, he tries hard but can't really make it— he hasn't really the success of a parrot. Of course he doesn't know this—he thinks he's done the trick all right. When he thinks of his present predicament, he puts it down to 'conditions' and 'bad luck.' The truth is he's had too far to go in the time, too little energy to make it. And on the whole he's far too nice a fellow to become the dream Diver. He's too tolerant; he spends too much time in trying to make people comfortable. He's got some natural *politesse*, brotherliness or something that blends into a cheery hail-fellow-well-met-ness. It might be a need for applause; but I don't really think so. Do you?

I felt as though something had been taken away from me:

—But the ladies? Surely he gets on with . . . ?

Bradford shrugged his shoulders, smashed the wet end of cigarette into an advertisement ash tray:

—Ladies? He's had a few, I suppose. But even there he doesn't concentrate hard enough, he gets too friendly. He doesn't even seem to see where the going's easy—there's that odd piece Norma after him just now, she's a new arrival to Number 48. She's fallen for Charley all right—God knows why, perhaps he looks pretty good at first, perhaps it's just because he doesn't respond. Hardly gives her a glance. Perhaps he's otherwise occupied—but whether it's with a woman or a garage the Lord alone knows. If you ask me, it wouldn't matter, you'd hardly tell the difference the old bags he seems to collect.

Bradford's voice had risen, his eyebrows had fixed their tufts savagely out towards me—they looked like the antennae of some warrior ant, while beneath the eyes began to blaze:

—Bags, Mr. Bishop. The sad residue of this crumbling borough, this decrepitous mark of Victoria's greatness, this haven for bags and hags and for spotted princes, students of the chassis and the parlors of aerated orange vice. You, Mr. Bishop, have I believe an establishment in the Parade called Seychelles?

I nodded automatically, I was counting over and over again that word 'bags.' Meanwhile Bradford went straight on. He stretched out one arm, one mackintoshed sleeve, keeping the other gripped on his beer:

—Seychelles Parade! And does anyone here dream of inquiring into that name? Into how it came there, into what it is—outside some vague memory from their battered old atlases? Inquiring—and finding it to designate no less than ninety glittering islands set like jewels in the blue tropical ocean of India: and the names, the names, Bishop, of those islands . . . Praslin, Silhouette, Curieuse, Félicité, Bijoutier . . . Rename your establishment, Monsieur Bishop, call yourself Maison Curieuse, Coiffeur de Seychelles Parade!

Now I was both angry and startled. It made me see his face very clearly, his pale eyes shone like soft metal in the veined rubber of his cheeks. He brought his voice to a crisis of exclamation—then suddenly slumped back into his wicker chair! He breathed heavily, sighed, deflated himself again. Then looked up wearily:

—You see? Poetry. But give me pencil and paper . . . I'm done . . . no good. No good at all . . .

He had crumbled absolutely. He looked more blown than ever, sunk in a bog of self-disfavor:

—And I should be talking of Diver and his lousy old women. . . .

I could say nothing, I was hot with resentment but there was nothing I could make my lips say—I had to hold back.

Then the swing doors opened. I saw them in the mirror, framed in frosted engraving, as though they were doors in some room beyond. And as in a dream framed in these doors the large gingerish-brown figure of a distant Charles Diver stood aside to admit a woman. She had a blond head. I stared harder—it was difficult to be sure—then I turned.

It was indeed the main door to this the saloon bar, and

there were Charles Diver and my wife. Already Charley was signaling a greeting. Madge's face was turned in the direction of the bar. Bradford said:

–But isn't that your missus? You didn't tell me she was coming?

I must have muttered something, it was as much as I could do to grip myself, to be ready, to appear pleased and casual. And before Diver said anything Madge was standing above me with a look of curious concern—was it fear or surprise?—which quickly dissolved into a greeting:

–Why, Henry! What on earth are you doing here?

–The waterworks, I was passing . . .

–And what am I doing here, for that matter? Fancy us meeting! Here! I just met Charley and he said come in for one, only one, and do you know I said I would?

Diver was standing above and twinkling his eyes down as though he had performed some especially clever trick:

–Met the missus by the bus stop, prevailed upon her to step in for a quick one—and what do we find, the errant husband at his cups! Waterworks is a good one—Hop-and-Cold Water, eh?

At which they all broke into laughter so loud that several people at the bar turned. I tried to smile. Could they have spent the afternoon together, was the arrangement with Madge's sister a covering ruse? The possibility loomed enormously as I tried to make my face smile. Diver went to the bar and brought back some drinks. Madge sat down on one of the wicker chairs—I remember watching her almost with hate, watching her settle herself, so absolutely, with so much easing and quiet flurry, piling her gloves and parcels in definite places on her lap, standing her bag firmly on the green-glass table top, sighing with brazen satisfaction—as though she were in some way

setting up house. This completed, she sat bolt upright
and said:

—Well, this *is* nice.

And while they all talked, Diver and Dicky and Richard
and Bradford, while the cigarettes passed and the smoke
rose and the glasses moved with beer, while the pink lampshades glowed darkly and the mirrors glittered dust and
the mackintoshes shuffled at the bar, while the cigarette
packets were screwed and the litter of stubs grew and the
ceiling light shone blackly on the clock—she hastened to
tell me in suspicious detail exactly what she had done that
afternoon. How her sister had rearranged the furniture
in the front room, how the lawn had grown inches high in
only a few months, how there had been burglars two doors
away. I watched her very closely, keeping my eyes fixed
on hers, convincing myself of her discomfort and feeling
a deep, hollow apprehension.

# 4

About three weeks later, I met Norma by arrangement at a bus stop in the West End. More accurately this was on the fringe of the West End, near one of the Northern railway terminus stations. A busy district, radiating all around the garish impromptu atmosphere that infects a neighborhood of large railway stations: buildings and shops and restaurants have a look of one-night-fair booths, an urgency and a shabby glitter that will soon have served its purpose and passed on. But that is only an atmosphere—my second shop was in that particular district, and it paid very well.

We shook hands under the red and white 'stop' sign, against a drab brown shop front—and I remember how spruce and vivid that girl looked against the drabness. She had on a tight tailored costume, there was about her an absolute neatness—she seemed hitched up everywhere beyond a possibility of ever loosening, her hair was tightly pinned, she wore those rimless glasses above the severely painted mouth, she offered a clean slim white firm hand with cold surety:

—I do hope I'm not late, Mr. Bishop. The manager was a bit difficult—it wasn't really my Saturday off.

–Not at all. It's exactly one o'clock—we go this way. How are you? . . .

I was hurrying her as quickly as possible away from that main street of people and crowded buses. I might have seemed flurried—she looked up at me quickly, glittering mascaraed eyes behind the rimless spectacles, but said nothing, perhaps acceding to my wish to be away from the highway as without question she had agreed to meet me in the West End rather than in our own neighborhood. I muttered:

–People talk so. But would you like a cup of tea, a sandwich? First?

–Well, really, I'm not hungry just now, not at all. Let's have a cup of tea after. I know a place where we can go and have a nice long talk.

She smiled and glittered up at me again with those glasses. She seemed utterly certain of herself, as certain as were the clothes she wore, severe but still feminine. Casually, as though it were a routine—though to me it felt so personal—she took my arm. I remember stiffening, looking quickly to either side. As we drew near the shop I took care to free this arm, pretending to search for something in my pockets.

Outside the street there was the wide free echo of mainroad traffic. But as soon as we opened the shop door the world of sound changed dramatically, violently—from the long cubicled room, a room full of very small partitions, there came a fierce constricted whirring, a hissing of jetted air and a spinning of small electric wheels, droning and rising, blowing it seemed and rinsing a million hairs upright in their follicles behind the lines of white rubber curtains. It always struck me forcefully—I never got quite used to this atmosphere of modern machinery.

White-smocked girls continually came and went between
the partitions whose secret occupants might for a moment
be seen immobilized, clamped into chairs before mirrored
basins and each wearing what looked like giant aluminum
crash helmets.

My manageress came forward. I introduced Miss
Norma Devereux, the young lady about whom I had telephoned. She was to be given a permanent wave, of a
special kind, after a fashion that she herself would specify.
I would go into the office. So that Norma was piloted into
one of the cubicles, the rubber curtain slid after her, and
she was gone. I went into the back room—and looked out
with relief at the quiet, dingy, unmoving back roofscape.
I had two hours to wait—alone with mixed feelings of
excitement, suspense, guilt, and achievement. Plenty of
time again to turn over in my mind all that had happened
recently; the habit had grown on me, a continual turning
over and turning over of things in the mind.

And much had happened. I had spent the three weeks
in cultivating an acquaintanceship with Number 48. I had
gone to work with care and some energy, swallowing small
rebuffs but capitalizing each opportunity most assidu-
ously. I had formed the habit of dropping in to the Claverton for a glass of beer—and I don't much like beer—
and more than once I had walked back to Number 48 with
Bradford or Richard Dawk, more than once accepted
their invitation to a further drink or a cup of coffee.
I had spared no pains to be pleasant, changing my
manner to suit one or the other of them. I had spared
no money either, I had offered drinks as freely as possible,
without seeming patronizing, but as an older and more
established man. They ordered beer—I was pleased to
offer them 'short ones.' And for two of the ladies—Mrs.

Lawlor and Norma—I managed to bring quite by chance in my pockets certain delicacies from the shop—combs, small bottles of brilliantine, particularly fine hairnets— and in a time of scarcity these were most successfully received.

At the same time I had seen to it that Diver and Madge and I met formally several times. Diver had twice been asked to dinner, once we had been taken for a drive in one of Diver's cars before returning for drinks at the Claverton and a cold supper in Diver's flat. Although this cost some anguish afterwards, I must confess that when I watched them together I was filled with a strange excitement. I felt in some sense superior—I had manufactured the situation, it was they who were watched and guilty.

I believe I began to enjoy the feeling of being the deceived, the unwanted, the injured. Sitting alone in the library, I used to take out the little key and open the small drawers where I kept those few notes I had made; read and reread them, then sit back and consider all over again the question of the house next door. More and more I thought of the two houses as a single entity, with a passage between but nevertheless joined—my purple-bricked romantic intricacy and the square, plainer edifice of Number 48 with its rain-washed flagpole and its black blind windows.

The house was, I now knew, owned by Mrs. Lawlor. She had bought it about two years previously—the money came from a legacy—turning it then into residential rooms. Only Diver had a complete flat, but that was because his part was the basement, the damp kitchens of the one-time mansion, and hardly worth dividing into rooms. To engage upon such a scheme had meant a great change in Mrs. Lawlor's life—hitherto she had lived on in her dead husband's house in a southern suburb. Then at a time when her income was much reduced and the cost of living rising, she had been saved by this legacy of some few thousand pounds. Feeling tearfully her descent in station, mourning her past leisure yet delighted that there should be an end to her loneliness, she had 'gone into business.' She ran the house with two daily maids. There were nine rooms, apart from Diver's basement. She herself occupied a second-floor 'best' bedroom; the others were let singly to students and business people, male and female. Of these Bradford, Norma, and the two boys Dicky and Richard constituted the intimate background that I had set myself to know. Bradford occupied a large room—that reeked, according to Mrs. Lawlor, of incense and sardines—directly above Diver; Bradford spent most of the days there. Dicky and Richard were both clerks, one in an estate agent's and the other in the accounts department of a rubber company. Norma ran the cosmetic department of a West End chemist.

From our first meeting I had known that Norma wanted something from me. She herself hardly dissembled the fact. What she wanted was fairly simple—it was the most specialized perm possible, and free. For this, it seemed, she was prepared to flirt, in fact to take me on at a certain remove as a sort of elderly admirer with a purse, a non-operative 'sugar daddy.' She could hardly have chosen a more disinterested gentleman: though as things turned out I had decided to play the part. In return for my nepotic interest, I would receive a niecely love, a succession of intimate smiles and a loving pat to the hair, a straightening of the tie and a hug of the arm: nothing further. Norma was a girl who claimed for womanhood much of its old pedestal; there was a primness and a seclusion about her not altogether denied by her bright cosmetics and certain sensualities of her clothes. I think that if anyone had suggested at this point that her relations with me might ever be advanced further than a squeeze of the avuncular arm, she would have laughed. She would have tapped her forehead with one of her long, thin, carefully scrubbed and glassily varnished fingers. For my part, I knew that Norma—if, as Bradford had said, she had 'fallen' for Diver—would probably be more ready than the others to speak of him; and she would know more, too.

Standing and staring out at the brown roofs opposite, such thoughts continued to turn, convolving, speculating, twisting about within themselves and darting off at all angles, exploring new ground, returning to the old— always, always moving. While downstairs in her cubicle my Norma sat, glinting contraptions humming round her, a copy of a motion picture magazine on her lap. The woman attendant in her white smock would have been leaning over her, in clean attendance, smoothing her into beauty. Bottles of soft preparations would glint on the basin in front, there would be an atmosphere of scientific refreshment and of smooth transformation in the air. Norma would look up at the mirror, see her face swathed, look down at the glossy face of some glum-lipped film-star —the finished product. The engines would hum smoothly. She would believe.

I looked at my watch, walked about the room. Three wax heads stood on a shelf; I remember taking out a comb and making adjustments to the blue hair on one of these. The wide fixed eyes stared, eternally concerned with the waxen thoughts within; I should think my own eyes stared back much the same way. The thoughts still turned.

And with the passing minutes turned faster—for today, and now in fact soon, was a day of special action. First tea with Norma, and as much as could be discovered. At five-thirty tea again—with Mrs. Lawlor. And afterwards, at a chosen moment, a moment subtly to be devised, a visit to Diver's flat. Diver would be out—there was a definite engagement, long talked about some nights ago, with some Old Boy's association, a dinner that Diver had advertised at length, boasting of his Old School Tie. With which he was that evening to be, I hoped, hoisted.

Norma settled herself on a comfortable settee against the mirrored wall, glanced once in the mirror, then sat upright with her straight back not touching the cushions. Away over the other tables, past pillars coated with rough new plaster, across a space of glistening dance-floor, a band shook out its slow brassy music—it coughed like distant golden coins. A waitress came and without smiling, without looking at us wrote down on a little pad the order, strolling away before I had even finished speaking. I had to raise my voice for the last words:
—And one tea with lemon.
—Lemon essence?
It was no question, but a statement; the waitress had moved far away without waiting for an answer. But Norma thoroughly approved of the place—she gleamed brightly with her spectacles.
—It's nice here, isn't it—I like the band. You can always dance. That's if you want.
I was still looking anxiously over the room for fear of seeing someone I knew—pretending to lean over to straighten the tablecloth so that I could peer round one of those many pillars—and muttered that I found it most

comfortable. Then Norma began to ask me a set of questions she had prepared on styles and methods of hairdressing; these I could answer easily—and meanwhile I had time to study her. She was, I soon decided, a type of girl whom for once I knew quite well—I employed several like her. Her all-consuming interest was beautification—her world was of varnishes and creams, astringents and lotions, unguents and oils and powders and perfumes. The newer they were, the more clinical the design of containers, the better she liked them. Hers was no study of quality but of novelty, so that a new cream approximated the latest film or dance tune. Films and jazz were secondary to this main cosmetic interest; for although the cinema's fabulous star creatures provided the dream paradise which in the first place stimulated these cosmetics, it had progressed beyond that; the cosmetic had become the real, practical means of approximating some resemblance to the star, and the star, though a guide, shone with a more distant and less urgent light. Since Norma was a girl of more than usual good looks, she was rather the less deeply affected by films, by the need for that paradise into which so many weekly entered. She could realize much of it in the mirror, and in the mirror of other people's congratulation. She spent a great part of her daily life talking of, searching for, and looking at various preparations—those usually on the open market, and thus possible and part of the game.

—What do you think of that tall girl over there with the fair boy, the girl in bluey-gray? She dances nicely, but do you think . . . She looks funny to me.

Norma was concentrated on the couple dancing past. The esoteric of differing faces, differing within limits known to her, held her absolutely. Her mind—it was

dreamily obvious—searched for a comparison among pho-
tographed star faces for these faces now passing. She
screwed up her forehead. I saw with astonishment again
how the eyes were most heavily made up behind these rimless, so neat glasses. They seemed thus unnecessary, some
sort of trick device. I suddenly thought—a fetish? And
of others with peculiar obsessions, of whom there were
not few to be met in my profession. Somehow this one
solution embraced Norma's whole appearance more easily
than any other. I was so startled that without thinking
I heard my lips saying:

—What do you think of Charles Diver?

Instantly I held my breath, wishing to have back the
words. But I need not have troubled—to talk of people
was so customary with Norma that she suspected no
secondary motive, only asked without meaning it:

—Why do you ask me?

And instantly continued:

—Charley's a very nice boy. *His* trouble is he's too set
on his business all the time. Mind you I'm not saying it
isn't worrying enough to have a business—not these days
—but then it can't be all of life, can it? I mean it's not
natural. I know Charley likes his bit of fun the same as
we all do. Don't we?

Then something extraordinary overcame Norma. It
may have been intuition; or a slow awakening of interest,
talking of people she knew rather than simply speculating
on the dream faces passing; or a sudden spur given her
by the memory of wished-for Charles Diver and the real-
ization of this poor substitute sitting before her. Because
now, with sudden insight and energy, with a stroke of
profound generalship—an absolute yet possibly uncon-
scious grasp of the tactical situation of personalities, a

feminine adroit generalship—she contrived three moods almost at once. As she said 'Don't we?' she glittered through her spectacles at me and emphasized the word 'we' so that again I felt, pleased and afraid, the flash of intimacy. Then she repeated, this time with sly curiosity and a look of defense:

—Why ask me?

And instantly on top of this she said:

—He's quite a one for the ladies, too. Seemed to be getting along well enough with Mrs. Bishop the other night, I must say!

She laughed then, trying to pass this off as fun. But then paused—and one could not be sure whether she was not intent on a fabrication, for she spoke slowly and carefully, as though testing her words as they made the sentence.

—That reminds me, they were out shopping this morning, weren't they? Having a coffee in Sangster's. Mrs. B. looked so smart, I thought, in her brown.

I said nothing. I tried to speak, but no words came. I seemed to remember that Madge had gone out early in a blue dress that morning; yet my imagination was working acutely, and always so confusedly divided between wish and distaste, that I could not be certain of this. But even then I noticed a gleam of success behind Norma's glasses as she saw her point strike home. I would have known at another time that this in itself was suspect, that such eager triumph was often the result of exaggeration; but now it concerned me—and I believed what she said. She drove her point further, instinctively understating.

—I do think it's nice for friends to meet and have a cup of coffee, I mean there's nothing wrong in that, is there?

Yet what would they have said fifty years ago! But now life's so much easier. I don't suppose you've known Charley long, he's only moved in a month or two back. That's really nice, people get together much more chummily nowadays, don't they?

Just then she reached for a cake at the same time as I reached for some sugar. Our hands touched. Norma left hers resting there a subtle second longer than was necessary. She looked up quickly, smiled an arch apology. I was thinking only of Diver's hand touching Madge's in that coffee room in the High Street—how long had those two rested together, how warm the touch, how much of a message?

A little later we rose to have 'just one dance.' Once again Norma did the unpredictable. Cool in her glasses, erect of back, modest and untouchable in her tall neck— as soon as she was in my arms she thrust her thighs against mine, clamping herself immovably. But her back arched away, and behind her glasses she looked as cool and distant as before—as if she were arranging flowers, cold irises in some empty room. I was shocked, tried to hum but of course I did not know the tune. I tried fiercely to remember some tango step of years ago, a step where the couple parted and walked for a little side by side; but it was so long ago, I had forgotten. So we continued as we were, our faces a foot or more apart, but interlinked as one body. Norma said:

—There's that girl in bluey-gray again!

And, surveying the room distantly, as equipment, as an engine for sport:

—A nice floor, nice and springy. Not too slippery either.

And then added, cold as a swan:

—Nice and spacey too.

At last the music ended. We separated. Several people clapped. I looked in despair at the bandstand. But it was over; the musicians with masklike faces were tiredly putting their instruments down by their sides, staring straight at the dancers who asked for more and without expression refusing to give it. Quickly I took out my watch:

—Heavens, ten past five! I'm very sorry, Miss Devereux . . . but I really have to go now.

—Must you really?

—I promised to have tea with Mrs. Lawlor at half past.

—Tea again! You're not by any chance fond of a cup of tea I don't suppose?

—Well, not as much as that! But I must get back now—do you mind?

—Well, I'm going home too so we can go together.

—Eh?

—Home to Number 48.

—Ah. Unfortunately I've a thing or two to do first. . . .

—Sure you're not scared of being seen with me?

—Scared?

—*I mean, there's nothing wrong in that, is there?*

I remember the words plainly, I thought I saw one of those glitterings again behind the impassive spectacles. I damned her for this, I damned her for suddenly being as frank as to suppose me 'scared,' I damned her for spoiling what had seemed so far a mutual tact, I damned her because also with all this I realized as we left the floor that I wanted to dance again.

We said good-by outside the tearoom. Norma held my hand a moment longer than might have been necessary, while looking away in another direction. 'See you soon?' was the attitude. And 'thank you for a lovely afternoon.'

I watched her walk away, tight and meticulous in bearing, walking with very short steps in her tight skirt. Then I turned quickly, walked round the corner and looked for a taxi.

Inside, all the way home, I thanked a providence that had saved Sangster's Tearoom in the High Street from having a morning dance at coffee time. And then shuddered to think that in any case there were afternoons unknown of, that such a meeting might have already occurred between Madge and Diver. How did Madge dance? I could not remember. The taxi trundled and curved on through the brown streets. Soon trees began to appear and we entered my district. I straightened my tie, I must indeed have straightened my mind too, for looking out of the window I saw a shop sign which gave me a sudden idea. I looked at my watch—half past five—and tapped the taxi window. Telling the driver to wait, I went into the shop and came out a moment later with a wrapped bottle under my arm.

We drank tea from black and gold *nouveau* teacups. I was keeping the VINTREX hidden until the moment should come, sometime after six, when Diver would be well clear of the house. It was quiet. I regained some composure watching the tired, pleading white face against the dark curtains—listening to her plaintive voice hushed in a room as still as the silver vases and the white trelliswork shining dully against a pale wallpaper flecked like granite. Mrs. Lawlor's old life had died; and among many photographs, some in silver frames, others in black-edged passe partout—gray-white pictures of long past babies and dogs and picnics and nephews and officers in early khaki— among the dark polished thin-legged tables, the white statuettes, the copper bowls, and all the other crowded miniature things placed exactly and each one polished immaculately and forever clean . . . it seemed that Mrs. Lawlor too was dead. Her hair was dyed coal-black, with her white face lined and tragic she sat always in the full light of the window; though nevertheless she contrived her own shadow. A dark mauve screen of silk and black wood by the door sealed this wistful columbarium, though perhaps rather than of mortal death over the room hung the softly cold light, the draped immobility, the death by shutter of the photographer's studio.

I did not dislike this. In a recuperative sense I was drawn towards such an atmosphere. A state of ill-resigned martyrdom pervaded Mrs. Lawlor; injured she was by the passing of her loved ones—and by the decline of her back, by the thoughtlessness of her lodgers, by the delinquencies of passing maids. She liked to smile and suppose that after all it was all for the best; but her lips quavered, her eyes shone with held-in wetness, her head was allowed to droop a little to one side as in the cold gray daylight she faced the window. Her back—and all the work she had to do, nothing but slave, slave, slave! But in my few visits I saw that in fact she did no slaving but spent the greater part of her time in her room among her 'artistic' trophies: but then she did a lot of sorting—sorting photographs, sorting boxes of cut-up 'stuffs,' sorting drawerful after drawerful of clean bric-a-brac. She never knew, she had to admit, when she would ever get straight.

And what did she think of her tenants, of Mr. Diver? Mr. Diver—*there* was a nice steady type. And hard-working—above all a gentleman too. He was, she had to admit, quite a help sometimes, quite the handyman if she wanted a shelf put up or a doorknob screwed. Though, she had to admit too, it was a little strange how on occasions he seemed to stay away all night—but then, that was none of her business, was it? She was sure he had *relations* to go to.

That Mr. Bradford was a different kettle of fish altogether. He was a queer one, a dark horse if you asked her. For the life of her she couldn't understand him. Of course, he was an author, and that explained a lot; but must he walk about on the front steps in his dressing gown? Must he wrap up all those rabbit bones in newspaper and put them under her bushes 'to see what the rain did'? Must he burn those messy little cones of incense all over his room—the room that smelt of incense and food and mackintoshes? But then of course one might say he was the understanding type, he was a man you could talk to; though sometimes you wondered if he was taking you quite seriously, you caught him *looking at you sometimes*. There are things I can't understand, Mrs. Lawlor said, wrinkling her face up, setting into motion several parallel lines on her forehead. (It never seemed to occur to her that these much-cried words *I can't understand* were in no way a statement of value but merely a straight confession of her own incompetence.) In the same way she simply couldn't understand Miss Devereux; you'd think a strong healthy girl like that might offer to help a little with things sometimes, but no, not a hand's turn. Her ladyship seemed to have quite a life of her own.

Not, of course, that she was saying anything against anybody. We lived in a free country, didn't we? And everybody could do just exactly what they wished. She was sure they were all good people at heart. In their own way of course. One mustn't grumble, one must agree that

everything was for the best, mustn't one? *She* was not
going to criticize. Still—there were one or two little
things one couldn't help noticing. *She* had no business to
condemn—but really, when you saw some of the things
that went on in this very house, right under her nose,
in *her* house, things that you wouldn't dream of if you
saw their melt-your-butter smiles afterwards, things that
nobody who wasn't brought up in a *slum* would do, why
you'd wonder where they *were* brought up, you'd wonder
if they weren't barbarians, hoodlums, yahoos. . . .

Mrs. Lawlor showed small signs of red all over her
face, it was as though the whiteness of her powder covered a hidden surge of blood. And her voice was rising.
I listened carefully and quietly, nodding and making
friendly noises with my cup and saucer and spoon, clinking things to show we were still there intimately together.
I listened with patience to a succession of small wrongs,
I was taken through the bathroom with its two separate
rings of shadow round the bath, its white toothpaste
splashed all over the cork floor, its towels left anyhow
and its mess of damp soap and powder; up and down the
stairs (the linen cupboards were right at the top and
one maid had simply refused to carry fresh linen all that
way down to Mr. Bradford—so she'd had to go); the
stairs which somehow carried mud right to the very top
and on which people thought they could throw cigarette
ends—why, she found two stale kippers on a plate on
the stairs once! And the rooms! The rooms with their
ash trays, their drawing pins stuck in the walls, their
dusty books, their locked drawers—nobody knew what
went on in those locked drawers—and that Norma for
instance had taken the two water colors of Windermere
right down off the wall and stuck the wall over with

photographs of, if you please, kinematograph stars. But
*then*, somehow or other, it was really a *clean* house, not
like some, and she, Mrs. Lawlor, liked to keep everything
spic and span even if it was sometimes a trouble and she
had to do it alone with only the two maids, girls who left
at six punctual every night as airy as you please!

To all this and much more I listened with care, trying
to note what I wished, forgetting most of it in the confusion. What did strike me, however, was that Diver himself was well liked, that Mrs. Lawlor for one had a soft
spot for him. Was this the result of Diver's insidious
diplomacy? Was he trying to keep on the good side of his
landlady, using his male attractions? I could put down
Mrs. Lawlor's distaste for Norma as secret jealousy,
something misplaced in so elderly a woman, but possibly
real and strong enough: it could be projected—Mrs.
Lawlor might think of Diver as a sort of son, a dear boy
to be mothered.

Suddenly she stopped, the redness left her face, her
voice lowered and became sweet and sad and again wistful.
She looked out over the roofs, out at the thinning daylight, at the empty serene light of a sun soon to die but
still bluely of the late afternoon. She sighed and tearfully smiled:

—But then, one mustn't grumble. I'm really very happy
to have them here. You see, now I'm never lonely any more.

This made me nervous. There had come into her face a
real seriousness, sincere beyond the wistful smile. Her eyes
had a practical look. I reached down to the floor where
I had placed the parcel.

—I took the liberty, Mrs. Lawlor, since you were so
kind as to invite me, to bring you along a little present.
Don't think me naughty, but I thought you'd like . . .

I had the beginnings of the wrapper off the bottle, its red stopper showed wineishly above the black glass. Mrs. Lawlor's lips tightened:

—I'm sure it's very kind of you, Mr. Bishop. But I seldom take a glass. I seldom have wine in the house at all, I really don't like to have it here. I think—don't you?—it would be best if you kept it, kept it for home.

She had risen from her chair and had walked slowly over to the window. There she stood, her profile towards me—and I saw then what seemed to be almost an aggressive display of disapproval. Her body she held up resolutely to its full height, her frail shoulders were fixed in an attitude of discipline, there was none of the sway and wave that usually her mauve clothes wistfully attained—she looked stern, admirable, like an elderly woman standing erect and painedly rigid for the National Anthem. I was awed, I had no idea such a simple gesture could have provoked this sanction, and I still held unmoved the bottle in my hand. Mrs. Lawlor's chin stuck forward, gripped by jawbones clenched tight in her cheeks. Her eyes stared straight out through the window. I lowered the bottle—and as I did this Mrs. Lawlor flinched. She must have seen the glint of that bottle from the corner of her eye. I apologized.

—I'm so sorry, I thought—it might do you good. . . .

Mrs. Lawlor glanced aside down at me. Her eyes saw also the bottle and I was disturbed to see a strange light in them.

—Thank you, but I think we will not open it here.

Her voice was slow, her lips weakened within the still rigid poise of her thin body. Of course I dismissed that small scheme of mine. To tempt the old lady would have been very wicked. I suddenly saw that she was not being

strict with me, but with herself—she was applying some
most difficult discipline. So I made what in fact was the
most unfair move of all. Quite sincerely I said that naturally we would not open the bottle, and started to re-
wrap the brown paper.

—Do you really think—it might do me good . . . ?

Mrs. Lawlor had moved over to me. She spoke quickly,
and with a sudden smile of ingratiation.

—Perhaps one glass, Mr. Bishop?

My hands were still folding the brown paper. It was
too much for Mrs. Lawlor. Had it been left there glinting
at her, then she might well have maintained, and perhaps
successfully to the end, her play of discipline. But to see
the bottle disappear sharply, definitely! With a gesture
of graceful ceremony, a restrained gesture but not one
to be denied, she reached forward her arm and grasped
the bottle-neck.

—Thank you, Mr. Bishop. Perhaps one glass.

It was quite plain from the extraordinary excitement
in her eye that this elderly woman was a real drinker—
and pathetically one who tried to stop. But I could hardly
snatch away the bottle. I just let it go—and black and
glossy it came like a clean-armored chrysalis from its
cocoon of brown wrapping. Mrs. Lawlor was already
off to a small closet by her divan-bed. She was talking
quickly, making sure that I had no chance to demand the
bottle back. The words streamed excitedly:

—Now just wait while I get two glasses they're in here
yes just here and we won't need a corkscrew so handy so
very handy these little stoppers that you can just just so
easily screw off with your own hand just—like—*that!*
There.

Before I had time to say a word, there with extraordinary efficiency was the glass in my hand. Ruby-red its
color, its wink of something rich and jeweled against the
dead mauves and grays and stone-white of the room falling
into dusk around us. One gleam of last sunlight patterned
itself suddenly on the frieze, far above the photographs;
it reflected in a mirror and caught in its refraction Mrs.
Lawlor's red polished glass as she lifted it, slowly, with
ceremonious slow delectation, to her smiling lips.

As soon as she had tasted the drink—first a sip and
then a long sip of half the glassful—I saw her most
noticeably appreciate. She sat more comfortably, upright
but more solidly, and looked round at the room with a
smile, very much like a lady sitting sipping her glass of
port on a Sunday morning in a public house, arrived to
enjoy herself and greeting all round with benign approval.
She began to talk brightly, cozily, nodding much and
speaking happily of her own little room, her friends in
the house, and of the nice neighborhood. I must say I felt
better at this. But she soon took another glass; and
another.

The time ticked away. Mrs. Lawlor still smiled happily,
but her speech grew slurred. She no longer looked out of
the empty window, inhaled the cold daylight—now she
was in the room, intimate and satisfied. I was worried.
But it was clear too that my action was irrevocable, I
could not now withdraw that bottle. And time was getting
on. There seemed to be no reason why I should not carry
on with my own affairs. So after a few minutes I rose
and asked Mrs. Lawlor if I might go downstairs—for a
moment? But of course I could, should she show me? No,
I knew the way.

✦

I went out into the darker passage. Mrs. Lawlor had the bottle and a drawer of bric-a-brac which with reminiscent nods she had begun to sort. It would be safe to remain away for some minutes—not too long, but long enough. So I went straight down the stairs to Diver's flat. It was easily accessible down the lower stairs, the old kitchen stairs. There was no interior front door.

Down below, in Diver's dark hallway, I hesitated. Silence. The coast was clear. But suddenly I stiffened. There had been a movement somewhere. Standing quite still I let my eyes follow the wall along, taking in the doors, the nests of disused pipes, the scabrous plaster patches, a coat hung shockingly for a moment human . . . and then saw what had not been there previously, a tank of goldfish. Red fish glimmered and moved behind their green glass. It had been no more than this. I went over and stood for a second looking at them. As many as about a dozen fish. Not like real fish—more like gadgets, just the sort of animal Diver would have liked. I dipped my finger into the tank; a blackish freckled fish darted away and disappeared into a tree of false coral, staying there then with its head hidden. Then I remember shaking my head, irritated at such dithering, and I hurried on into Diver's garden room, that room of the electric-eyed dogs and the false flowers and the courtyard peppering of dwarfs.

I went round the center table, on the side away from the blue airplane, and straight to the bureau standing by his French windows. These windows had been left open. A scent of flowering lime came in, and a rich under smell of thick motor oil and cleaning rags. Diver had been dismembering another car just outside the window to the left; now some of the parts stood in odd attitudes, like separate beings, on the smooth stone paving. I began opening drawers in the desk.

A desk of light-colored thin wood; the drawers scraped and stuck. I tried to move more carefully—but I was also careful of the time, for upstairs Mrs. Lawlor must soon look up from her sorting, remember my empty chair, and with blind happy eyes come searching the passages. I had to hurry. In the first drawer receipts and a few letters in typescript, automobile insurance papers. One drawer down a mixture of steel and aluminum screws and bits of small machines, wing nuts and valves. The next drawer, socks. On the other side, in the bottom drawer a thick wad of magazines—film weeklies, monochrome nudist papers. I fingered these with diffidence, they seemed all the more trash and obscene for a slight wish to turn their pages. But at the same time I shrank from the secret sensuality they revealed—I saw Diver feasting on them alone in this room, I remembered Bradford's vision of the lady models. That drawer I slammed shut angrily; the noise broke like a gunshot in the silence, I pulled myself together and went quickly to the next drawer above—a tin of biscuits, unused Christmas cards, pipe cleaners. Pipe cleaners! I remembered that other day of searching in my own house and the smell of pipe smoke in the empty kitchen. I took one of these white-furred sticks and put it in my pocket—and then from the next drawer took two things. One a snapshot of Diver on some holiday beach, in a bathing costume; the other—and with this in my hand I stood for a moment very still—a lipstick. It was of a kind that I knew Madge used—I remembered the gilt plastic holder with its three black rings. I placed it carefully in my waistcoat pocket and approached the center drawer. It looked the most important. I felt it would guard the most important. I felt it would guard the central secret. But I was never to open it.

I have a clear vision—at this remove of time—of that old house on that still evening. Empty, but for the two of us. Myself downstairs fingering hungrily at the drawers, the old woman upstairs with her half-finished bottle and her room of dead photographs sorting the beads in her basket. Two thus separate, each alone, each in a quiet room all alone, each nervously absorbed in his intimacies. The solemn white façade with its black window squares, its flagpole, its arid gravel drive must have stared emptily across to the plane trees, the broad tarmac avenue, the red gothic house opposite: inside there would have been no movement, only sometimes a shadowed flicker from two only of all those rooms. Staircases in between waited vacant, passages stood still. Clocks might have ticked and moved, but little else—perhaps a paper fluttered by an open window, perhaps a petal fell. And we two people, she of the faded eyes and the fingers dreaming their lost dreams among the beads, myself of the excited hands searching among forbidden things—both of us moving quietly, as quietly as the goldfish, only violent within.

But in that house there was a third figure—and this I saw suddenly through the French windows. I stopped, stooped rigid—searched for this figure which suddenly I knew was there, but could not exactly see. A second before I seemed to have seen it. Then again I caught it—in the detached glass windscreen of a car propped against the sundial there stood reflected, motionless, the figure of a man. Dark and glassy in the windscreen lay reflected blue of the sky and a picture of the façade of the house above

—though mostly of the veranda rail just above that garden room itself. The figure was standing with its hands to its sides, right against the white curled iron and creepered rail; it wore a dressing gown; its face seemed to stare directly down into mine; it was Bradford.

It seemed as if he was leaning forward, peering into the windscreen's reflection . . . he kept so still, suspiciously quiet. Could one see into a room? I was not far in—my head was over that narrow desk no more than a foot from the open window; I was in light. The possibilities flicked up and down like signal tabs—I felt trapped from behind, too, as though Mrs. Lawlor was already descending the stairs. They were terrible seconds. At first I kept dead still. Then the idea came to brazen the thing out, as much at least as I could . . . it was better than being caught. I edged the drawer closed with one knee—then straightened and waved a hand. But as I waved, at exactly that moment, the figure so intimate in the dark, moon-colored glass turned and disappeared. It was exactly as if he had refused the wave, as if he had turned in disgust. Excuses piled into my mind. That I had lost a fountain pen the night of that last cold supper, and was taking the liberty . . . ? I had wished to borrow some motoring magazine and reread the article Mr. Diver had so interestingly discussed? That I . . . but these all seemed wrong, I had searched too hard at the desk.

Then all I wanted was to get away quickly. I turned and was already mounting the stairs to the hall when a shadow came across the light at the top. Mrs. Lawlor's voice came:

—Oh, Mr. Diver, I didn't know you were in! I was looking for Mr. Bishop, he couldn't have come down to yours, could he?

A pause. She was now distinct, she had moved into the light and I could see the side of her face with one eye staring down hard. But the stairs were dark. I took a chance, feeling ridiculous, like a boy awkwardly playing a difficult game, and lowered my voice to resemble Diver's. I remember speaking in staccato, disconnected words:

—Not here. Excuse. Must be off.

Mrs. Lawlor bent closer:

—But I really don't know what could have happened, all the doors of the conveniences on the way down seemed open and . . .

—Must go. Hurry.

I stamped heavily on the stairs, trying to weigh as heavily as I could, but on my toes to make myself tall. I prayed the wine might have confused her, and edged suddenly against the wall. I listened, breathlessly again— and heard Mrs. Lawlor mumbling to herself. Then she moved away, there was a shuffling like slippers along the corridor above. But for a few minutes I stayed still, a leaden sense of catastrophe gathering in me. I stood just by the goldfish. Those quiet creatures in their tank swam slowly from coral to coral, sometimes rose horizontally as if in lifts. They were the only discernible objects in that gloom, I looked at them hard, waiting. Then, quiet as the fish themselves, I crept back up the stairs. Not a sound. I stopped and listened again in the hall.

Mrs. Lawlor was halfway up the main staircase, on a little landing, paused outside a door paned with frosted glass panels:

—Ah, there you are, Mrs. Lawlor!

—Why, I was just wondering where . . .

She hesitated, not liking to seem inquisitive—she remembered my errand had been a delicate one. She was at a loss and so I pressed her, the better to hide my own discomfort:

—You were just wondering where . . . ?

—I was just wondering whether the front door was closed. I went down.

—Ah, then you saw it open?

—No, it was closed.

—But Mrs. Lawlor—I've just closed it. I went out for a moment on the porch, I thought I saw my wife passing and went out. If you'd closed the door I couldn't have got in, could I?

—Oh.

—I know. It must have been just shut to. It must have looked shut.

—Ah, *that* must be it. Shut to.

She was relieved. Then I saw what a ridiculous risk I had taken—she might easily have tried the door on the way upstairs—and so now I too was relieved and laughed nervously, sealing the matter.

But the matter was not sealed. I could not leave it alone.

—I saw Diver going out. From the front steps.

—Oh, you saw Charley Diver? I just had a word with him at the top of his stairs. He must have come back.

—Yes, he must have.

But as we turned into Mrs. Lawlor's room again, I realized my mistake. This was exactly the kind of minor incident that might be mentioned again by anyone of Mrs. Lawlor's parochial mind, she whose parish was her house. So I went on quickly, stumbling out the words:

—Well, I wouldn't be sure it was Diver. It looked like him.

And this too was a mistake. Mrs. Lawlor instantly showed through her vagueness a sudden alarm:

—Then who could it have been? Who could it have—you don't think it was a *stranger*, a *man* . . . ?

I reassured her quickly. Of course it was Diver, it must have been. But now she persisted—and with apprehension I saw the bottle of VINTREX was empty.

—Oh dear, though . . . we'd better look, we'd better go down. . . .

She was already moving towards the door, she was bent on facing this, she must have been a courageous old woman. So down the empty stairs again we walked, Mrs. Lawlor leading. She had picked up none of those weapons one might have supposed, no poker, no stick—her only armament, as before when she fought the VINTREX, was a straightening of the shoulders, a rheumatic erection of her spare frame and her moral resources.

We searched Diver's flat and of course found nothing. But Mrs. Lawlor found the goldfish. For some seconds she stood before this tank, looking at the fish with suspicion. At length she said:

—I didn't know about these fish, I have a rule—no pets. I don't quite know about fish. But I'll speak to Mr. Diver about them, I'll speak about these fish.

She paused, and added strongly, as though this new matter of the fish tank prompted her:

—And I'll speak about this evening, I'll ask him whether he *was* here.

I said nothing. In a sudden panic, wanting above all else to be out of the house and away, I made my excuses and left.

# 5

My wife sat on a stool in front of her dressing table.
It was ten o'clock, night—a rift in the drawn curtains
showed the darkness outside and a patch of pale green
where a street lamp shone among the plane-leaves. Inside
it was all peach colored light and the brittle clean shine
of blue silk. As she brushed her short blond hair, she
smiled. The three mirrors reflected those amused deep
dimples, dimples like soft keen cuts. Playfully she called,
through the mirrors, in that embarrassing private lan-
guage:

—Boocles!

—Yes?

—Come bruss Maddie's hairs?

I looked up at the figure of my wife. I had been deep
in foreign thoughts of her. Now I came out of this preoccupation with an imagined Madge—a Madge in brown
sitting in Sangster's Tearoom—and saw the real figure
sitting only some feet away. A familiar figure, friendly
and lovable in its familiarity. In its cream silk slip, with
its other more intimate shoulder straps emerging on
the plump rough pink shoulders, in its enclosure of silk

elasticked drawers that now sat solidly on the stool, rich
in buttock, drooping this slightly over one side of the
stool. I saw all this with affection: then remembered it
was the same body that had appeared that afternoon now
long ago in the bathroom window; I swallowed the hopeless
pang that caught me. I just followed her tone—saying
something like:

—Maddie want her hair brussed?

—Es please.

—Wait little moments then.

She smiled three times at me from the triptych mirror,
making her eyes look upwards coyly at a curl fallen on
her powdered forehead. The mirror was all glass and
light, her face floated there like a stage face isolated.
I hitched up the suspender I had just undone and
got off the bed. As I walked over to her I stooped
slightly—I had never been able to walk about quite unself-
consciously in my underclothes. And the bedroom itself
always discomforted me. But I went over to brush Madge's
hair, not immediately in her mood, but knowing it well
enough and slipping easily into that absurd baby talk.
I had decided to use the moment for my own purpose.
As I took up the brush I said:

—Maddie's golden hair looks pretty?

—Pret?

—Lovely gold color. Maddie likes pretty colors?

—Mmmm. Red, green, blue.

—Brown?

—Oh, noooo. Brown nasty dull color.

—Maddie got pretty brown frock. Boocles favorite frock.

—Favert? Mmmmmm.

—Maddie never wears pretty brown frock.

—Yes, Maddie does, Boocles *fib*.

—No, no, never.

—Maddie wore brown fwock last week.

—Oho! When?

—Lemme see, Mudday? Tooday? Wen'day?

She was holding out one hand and ticking off the fingers as though they were little piggies going to market. She frowned, pretending the seriousness of a child. I waited behind, watching carefully the fingers, waiting for Saturday. In that triptych mirror the fingers appeared three times; in the bright light dizzying, fifteen fingers that counted towards Saturday; and behind, Madge's face and cream-wrapped bosom—and my skinny veil of white airtex. Now that the question had been broached, that baby talk was more difficult—I found it unusually absurd. But as Madge now suddenly stopped at Friday I managed to continue:

—F'iday, Maddie? Little birdie said Maddie look nice like pies in her bwown fwock on Sat'day.

—Sat'day?

She turned and looked straight up at me, plainly interested. The coyness went and she asked in her ordinary voice:

—Someone told you I wore it on Saturday? Who, Henry? That's very curious because I remember I wore my blue on Saturday. Henry, who?

I watched her face very closely while I hesitated for an answer. It showed nothing but the usual interest at the thought of people talking of her. So I temporized:

—Aha!

—Oh, do come on, don't be silly. Tell me, dear.

—Well . . . as a matter of fact it was the cashier in Sangster's.

—Sangster's? But I haven't been near there for a week.

She might have seen me in the street, of course. Though she's wrong about Saturday, it was Friday. But, Henry, what on earth were you doing in Sangster's?

—Me? I was—passing and dropped in for a coffee.

—On Saturday, Henry? I thought you went to town?

—No, the Monday after.

I must have let my face drop. Already I had decided Madge was lying, and ruthlessly lying without shame because she turned right round on the stool and faced me fairly and frankly. She began to talk in a wondering voice, wondering yet motherly, a voice of care. She started:

—Darling, what *is* the matter? Henry, is something the matter? I've been wondering—you've been quite strange these last weeks. What is it?

—Me? Nothing, nothing.

—But you don't seem at all your old self. You never go round and see George Patterson like you used to, you've missed the Stamp Club, I haven't seen you pick up a book once . . . Is there anything on your mind, dear?

—No.

—But there must be something.

—Well, as a matter of fact . . .

—Yes?

—I didn't want to worry you. But it's the shop.

—Oh, Henry dear—what is it?

—There's nothing exactly disastrous or . . .

—Disastrous! You *should* have told me, dear. What is it? Tell me *all* about it.

—Well . . . it's—like this. Things have been dropping a bit. Not much, but there's a decline. I had a talk with them at the Parade, he says he's doing his best with the shop but we've simply got to modernize. There isn't enough custom of the old sort left to keep things up to scratch. In fact, I've been thinking . . .

—Yes, dear?

—That I ought to take a more active hand for a few weeks. Not in the shop, but going round and seeing what's the state of things elsewhere. For instance, there are a couple of conventions coming up soon, and there's the Creamolin haircutting competition. That's in Liverpool. And the wholesalers, they aren't all in London you know: we're probably missing some good brushes and stuff. And machinery, there's a new drier in Coventry just now, I've heard it's already in the finishing stage up there at this moment.

—I see.

—I can't send any of the staff away, they're not dispensable even if they haven't got their hands full. It would just be a question of going myself.

—But you haven't made up your mind? Why?

—Oh, Madge, you know as well as I do, I've tried these last years to let the shops run themselves. You know me and business, we make a fair living like this and it's much easier.

—But, Henry, if it's going to fail, that's a different matter?

—It looks so.

—But then you *must* take a hand, darling. It sounds serious, I don't really understand these things, but it does sound, doesn't it?

—It'll mean me being away for a few days at a time.

—Neverthe*less*.

—A couple of nights perhaps.

—But if it's so necessary . . .

—But you'll be here alone.

—Don't be silly.

—I don't like leaving you. Here. There's only Enid, and she wouldn't be much good if . . .

—Now, Henry, put that out of your mind. *I* shall be all right.

—Hm.

—I shall be *quite* all right. Now——not another word!

I walked over to the other end of the room, to where the bedclothes were turned down revealing two pillows clean and white, and like two people. All I had said was based on truth; only my intentions were a lie. For some time I had planned to make some excuse to stay away— in fact to give Madge her head and then return suddenly. However—I had not counted on the ease with which Madge had accepted the proposal, she seemed to me far too ready to accept it. Too ready to have the house to herself. Too ready for me to leave her. Crushingly that childhood tearful feeling of being left out came over me again, I felt that dreaded hopelessness of exclusion. But I turned round to say:

—I'm glad you do see it that way. I thought you might be frightened alone. Now I'll go into the matter, see what's the first move to make.

Madge was finishing her hair. She left the dressing table and herself came walking over to the bed. She was smiling, consideration and love were in her eyes—she spoke soothingly, as though I were a child who had to be reassured. And as she got into bed she reached out her arm:

—Boocles, don't worry *any* more.

The dimples cut deep into her cheeks. Her lips pouted to make a soothing sound, a long deep groan like a repressed kiss.

–Look at silly Maddie—her hairs are all mussed again! Never mind, come to Maddie, come . . .

I let her take the sleeve of my pajama jacket and pull me gently into bed. I switched out the light. We lay close together. Madge continued to make those soothing sounds, maternally, in the dark. I felt the warmth of her body against my hand, the shape of her flesh as I put my arm round her: but then my hand was Diver's hand, and the darkly sensed shape the same that Diver might feel, this body I knew so well yielded now not to my touch but to Diver's. So as we made our love, as the soothing died in her throat, I tortured myself with a rediscovery of her body through Diver's red-haired arms—this thing once so much mine it seemed was stolen forever.

A little later, when she was asleep, and her breathing by my side rose and fell like a warm wave in the darkness, I lay on my back with eyes wide open. I began to cry. Silently, still with wide-open eyes. I cannot remember stopping.

I was speaking in a stern voice, quiet and definite:

–All right, Diver—it's time now for me to speak. Listen carefully. For some time now I've been watching you. I know quite well how you've been behaving, and don't suppose I don't. You're doing a damnable thing—you're putting yourself between a man and his wife. That man is me and it's my wife you're after with your sneaking attentions. I'd like you to know something—Madge and I have been married for nearly twenty years, we've been happy, nothing has come between us. Not until now, when you with your filthy backhand ways come sniveling in to make up to her, trying your best to turn her head with your cheap Casanova tricks. Behind my back, of course.

But what does Mr. Diver care for a lifetime's happiness? What do *you* care what sort of trust and faith you leave spoiled forever? As long as *your* vanity is satisfied? As long as *you* can add another to your list of successes? As long as *you* can satisfy your mean, contemptible lust? Look at you—you're not fit to touch her shoes, you disgusting red-headed swine, you beer-swiller, you cheap swine. Yes, I know you're stronger than me but see here— if you try any of that stuff I can still give as good as I can take. No. You're going to hear *me* out this time. Listen! Don't you ever *think?* Don't you ever imagine for a moment what you're doing to other people's lives with your filth? Don't you see what you're breaking? Don't you? Answer me. Answer!

I pressed my lips together and raised my voice:

—A moment's fun for you—and two people's lives ruined! And what do you care? You haven't a word to say, have you? Sneaking backdoor tricks—I saw you spying at my wife through the bathroom window. And don't think I don't know what's been going on since. I've got the evidence all right. Let me tell you. *I* know my wife was wearing brown that Saturday, *I* know there was a lipstick in your desk, I know there was . . .

My voice trailed off. I was quivering with anger, it seemed the words would never come. But there was a good reason—there were no words more, there was no more evidence, I had nothing to throw up in Diver's face. And in the room there was absolute silence. The figure facing me, a great black mantel clock with tarnished gold pillars, had long since ceased to tick.

It was the most imposing furniture in the little room, a room in a district a mile or two south of my own house.

I had rented it while I was supposed to be away on a business trip.

I was supposed to be in Liverpool. Instead, at seven o'clock in the morning, I stood shaved and dressed and alone in that bare little room. I had risen early, I was due to return home to Briarwood. I wanted to be early enough to catch them, at eight o'clock. Not too early to appear violent and suspicious—but normally early. It was a quarter of an hour's bus-ride away. I had to wait for a while. And now as my voice trailed away I saw again, with an angry sense of frustration, that with all I had done there was still little concrete evidence. I knew well enough myself. But that was the sum of small observation, there was no certain circumstantial clue. I stared vacantly at the black-leaded grate, at the sooted quill of white paper in the empty fireplace. Outside a milk cart rattled by. There was a beating of morning mats. Through the lace-trimmed window the tattered brown street resumed a daily round foreign to me. I had chosen this district particularly because there was no chance of being seen by any acquaintance, it was foreign to my way of living, alien though only a mile farther south than my own more prosperous residential borough. And yet I could walk down the low-storied severe straight street, cross a main road, climb a small hill between windowless warehouse walls to a widening place where a market of barrows was assembled—and from this dingy eminence I could see the flashing green of the waterworks' cupola.

In the fresh morning air, in the still room without fire or light, in that motionless new gray daylight I sat and stared at the black lead. After a few minutes, long minutes, I remember my eyes moving nearer to my boots. Nothing stirred—but in the stone-set solitude I suddenly grew conscious of my living body. Inside those black boots there were feet and toes and on the toes grayish-yellow hairs. There was a corn on one toe, a patch of hard skin along the side of the other foot. Inside the boot, inside the sock, there was life. And in this knowledge I understood clearly how all the time, motionless in a motionless room, my body was slowly, slowly falling to pieces. A gradual, infinitesimal disintegration was taking place. Nothing could stop it. Pores that once had been young were now drying up, hairs were loosening in their follicles, there was an acid crusting the backs of my teeth and my stomach. And what horrors persisted in the unseen entrails, among all those unbelievable inner organs? My fingernails were growing, phlegm accumulated itself on the membranes of my throat and nose—all the time steadily, relentlessly, a quiet change was taking place, the accelerating decadence of forty-five years. A gradual dismemberment—as the thought set those years themselves in menacing black figures before my eyes. I felt suddenly the suspicion that all was finished. Never to do this again, never that. Except —how rapidly one thought invoked another!—that there was still a chance. A last chance before some final impotence. Instinctively I reached forward, picked a box of matches from the mantelpiece, stowed it safely in my pocket. But a last chance of what? Of romance? But I wanted no one but Madge. Travel? But again—I was content at home with my habitual small pleasures. Yet . . . something else, there was a need for some other unstated self-assertion. To take, for once in life, action? To do something even violent, to rage once and shout my voice out to the skies, the streets, people? Before I grew too old, before I died? I was still young, at forty-five I felt thirty-five. I had time and indeed now was the time.

And the time was already then twenty-five minutes to eight. I got up suddenly, began pacing the small room—between the unmade bed with its shabby quilt and the wardrobe mirror alive with copper and indigo flecks.

But as fast as such an urgent thought possessed me, it was diminished; it rose like great music, swelling all hope and imagination—then fell quietly away. Such chords must indeed have been difficult to sustain in a heart as ordinarily composed as mine—they simply appeared and then sank into the softer music of my most habitual life. Still—the theme remained interwoven with the main music of life, in counterpoint it was softly stored. It might be joined with others of its kind, it might accumulate so that in time, towards the end of the piece, this new music accumulating might drown the old. But for a moment it diminished, took its latent place in the score.

I paced the room for the last few minutes, the old thoughts took possession, through my head raced again those many cries and responses that had occupied it for the last two days. Should I go and have it out, all cards on the table, with Madge? It was really extraordinary that I had so far contained myself! But from the thought of 'having it out' I as instantly shrunk—it would involve not only a possible denial, even scorn, even laughter, and in any case a sacrifice of my own vanity in admitting such a situation. And also—I can see it more plainly now—it involved a surrender of the situation: I was hurt, yet somehow I was delighted in this, I had an absorbing infirmity. It was too strong and evident to be passed over.

The scenes I enacted with Diver were part of this. They were many and most varied. I had taken to talking out loud—my tormented brain had to find relief in words. From the stern patriarchal upbraiding to a damn-it-all

down-to-earth it's-got-to-be-stopped-as-man-to-man; from
a sincere openhearted appeal to Diver to leave us alone,
to a tearful, beggarly prostration of myself before that
man's mercy. Again, I would engineer a curious mood of
generosity, a mood of sweet reasonability—after all if
Diver was after Madge then both he and I had the same
taste, the fellow couldn't be such a bad sort after all.
But then contrarily the hot blood of indignation would
rise, I would curse this intruder who vainly took it on
himself to mess up our lives. This, in its turn, would be
followed by an apathy of self-pity, when I would indulge
myself in my injury, when I would dream the sweet past
into a long-lost euphemy, a golden age now irrevocably
lost. I managed to conjure up all sorts of sweet happen-
ings, graceful moments not remembered in years; and now
all these were gone . . . it was extraordinary how definitely the door was shut, how sharp a difference was made
by the touch of another man's hand. Or of another man's
eyes—for of all things it was the delighted eyes of Diver
that I remembered most, those pig-blue eyes under the
ginger hair looking up at the bathroom window and the
body within. This picture—it was indeed the only precise
picture I yet had—recurred constantly, and it was the
worst of all, this vision of the body.

And in extenuation of this picture I saw again and
again, against varying scenes and in every light of day
and night, the deep red bladder of Diver's face, the pendu-
lous sac heavy with bad blood. And the papered whiteness
of his unclothed limbs, ginger-haired sunless skin that
might have crept out from the blind darkness under a
stone. But nevertheless a body hard with square muscle,
thick and tough beneath its light freckling. Slightly fawn
the skin grew where creases were, and the red stopped

at his neck and wrists sharply in a line drawn by collar and tight cuffs. And in this frame always the vain exultant mind was set, the victorious lecher winking through his blue pig eyes and the wet loosening of such a self-congratulatory mouth. Bristles of hog strength on his cheek to grit against Madge's skin, long mustache hairs to catch in the blond of her temples.

Image thus encouraged image, every intimacy could be imagined and then always improvised upon, there was a torture in feeling again Madge's old caresses and placing these in Diver's arms. But a torture curiously enjoyed. No sensation of horror and disgust, as when a wound is seen and quickly turned from; but instead a ceaseless reiteration of each imagined scene, a glossing of it and a molding, an effort made that it should linger as a motion picture might be held suspended, a tasting of it and a fascinated search for ever greater possibilities. Sometimes I shuddered, almost turned away with dread—but then was drawn back to peer again. I took my wife's place, yet as in a dream standing apart and still seeing her—how could she respond to such advances, how close her eyes in such quiet submission?

And then I caught at myself, at my own morbid pleasure—how could I bear to think of these things and taste them, like a man tasting the vertiginous distance of the precipice? I felt disgust at myself, accused myself of cold-blooded introspection—and from this proceeded instantly to condemn myself anyhow of playing an underhand game: spying, prying, sneaking. Two wrongs not making a right. In deceiving the deceiver, I was acting in a mean, ungenerous manner. Then as suddenly I saw Madge's face smiling at me in that coy manner from the bedroom mirror— a smile and a posture that so often I had dearly loved—

and now stopped suddenly shocked that she should at all be capable of such an expression of coquetry.

I stood suddenly stock-still in the middle of that chilly morning bedroom. Then quickly drew out my watch. It was already a quarter to eight! Those drumming thoughts —I was already five minutes late. I grabbed my suitcase and hurried out and down the stairs. I heard sounds of a tin basin and running water from the pale light at the kitchen end of the passage. There was a smell of linoleum and cooked cabbage. I remembered I had not settled the bill. Now there was no time. I hesitated a second, then clicked open the front door. The fresh gray air, the cold energy of the morning—at that moment a heavy furniture van rumbled past, a sound and shape that lumbered up, filling the street. I felt the noise pour past me into the passage. I shut the door quickly behind me. Down the street, not daring to look behind. But when I got on the bus the shadow still lay behind—such a small mistake to make, a bill I would certainly pay. But would the old lady downstairs search the room, find perhaps a dropped letter, some clue to my address? And would she then not write but with the direct anger of her kind come boldly and call?

I got off the bus at the next stop, I looked for a post office, was misdirected and then directed to a small grocer serving as a post office on the corner of a side street. There I had to wait—behind an office boy buying endless sheets of stamps—before I could get the postal order and the stamped envelope. By the time I had posted it, it was already twenty-five minutes past eight. I chanced a short cut back to the main street and the buses. It was a cul-de-sac. I had to trace my whole previous path back. By the time I ascended the next bus, it was twenty minutes to nine. On the bus I began thinking: Suppose the post failed, suppose I had written the wrong number?

It was thus nearly nine o'clock when I left the bus and began the short walk to Briarwood. I approached from an unfamiliar direction—and it happened to lead me past Diver's new garage.

In a row of dark plaster houses washed a leaden deep gray the astringent yellow garage broke its bright little wasteland. It was painted the hard yellow of cheap toys, a merciless bright color that took upon itself neither shading nor shadow. In its forecourt and in the gaping windowless front to its inner workshop lay the only dark relief—but this was the darkness of oil-smeared asphalt, of greenish-black pools, of cindered carbon, of the mineral dark dust of machines. Green petrol pumps stood out in this oily arid country, white notices with black and scarlet thin letters proclaimed prices and horsepowers; several unpolished cars stood about, empty creatures with no number plates, tired stuff due for grazing on the scrap heap.

From the inside, as I drew near, there came a metallic whirring—lathes must have been at work. The splutter of an electric self-starter, a hammer struck on some resounding tin sheet. Diver came walking quickly out and began to busy himself with one of the notices, blacking out what might have been too energetic a price. It was a shock to see him. I knew I was late. But somehow he should not have been there.

As I passed he looked up, stared for a second without smiling, then quickly looked down, flicking self-consciously at the board. I had been hurrying, hoping rather that he would not see me—but now I stopped. It was a surprising silence on the part of so usually buoyant a man. Something had happened? Silence of guilt?

—Nice morning!

Diver hesitated, then slowly looked round. He pretended then to see me for the first time.

—Oh . . . Henry . . . hello. Yes, rain's holding off.

His face suddenly turned up to the skies. As he screwed up his eyes it looked like an effort rather to avoid mine. A pause. Then I said:

—Up early this morning? I didn't know you garage proprietors got down to it so early.

—Had to get along earlier this morning.

Another pause. He looked up at the sky again, then down at his shoes. He was plainly embarrassed by my presence. But such was the pause, and such his expansive nature, that Diver had to look up, this time with a weakly forming smile:

—Yes, early bird this morning. Not often here before ten, but circumstances, you know. Force of circumstance, eh?

—Ah.

—Hello, what's the suitcase—human hair? Been away yourself?

For a minute or two more we talked—of the hairdressing competition, of Diver's garage. But it was plainly difficult for Diver, he was hiding something—though he made every attempt to force a weak joviality. He soon excused himself—and went away leaving the showcard half finished. I turned thoughtfully down the road. The grimness of execution struck me—this was after all what I had expected and now it had happened. I remembered the time and hurried—over an hour late, probably too late to detect any traces, and that after wasting two whole days in preparing for this sudden homecoming. But I turned the front-door key very quietly and slipped in without a sound.

Madge was on the stairs, fully dressed and in her hat. She looked at me with eyes widely opened, as at some catastrophe (though perhaps with no more horror than she normally expressed when something in the daily schedule became disarranged—a mistake in time or the method of a journey). She screamed:

–Henry!

–Hello, Madge. Morning.

–Henry, you said you were coming this evening, not this morning, what's happened, has anything happened, why didn't you tell me, you said this *evening?*

–I simply changed my plans, traveled overnight with the Creamolin people. We had a lot to talk about and there wasn't time in Liverpool.

–Well, you might have let me know.

–Why?

–Why? Well, there's—there's no harm is there in letting me know? I mean, now there's lunch to think of.

–I should have thought there were hours till lunchtime.

–Still . . .

–You're up early, if I may say so.

–I wanted to get to the shops.

–This early? Strange.

–I don't suppose *I* can change my mind once in a while, can I?

–Is anything wrong?

–Wrong?

–I mean, you sound cross.

–I'm sure I'm not cross.

–Then it must be my mistake.

–I'm sure it must be— Oh, Hen, don't let's be silly, come kiss Maddie.

She came down the last remaining stairs and towards me with her arms outstretched. I had been setting my bag on the floor, and now stooped and looking up at her wanted to shrink away—how could I kiss those lips already kissed? Everyone up so early. Everyone on edge. I made a cold effort to control myself, rose, submitted to the kiss, returned it with an awkward peck.

–Don't worry about me, go along to the shops now you're up.

–But I want to hear all about it, Hen. And what about your breakfast, have you had your breakfast?

–I had some on the train. Just you run along, we'll talk about that later.

–Oh, but I'm in no hurry to get out, not really.

I wanted to be alone, it had been necessary indeed to see her but this had been enough. I looked hard into her face, searching for guilt or shame. But found none. There was enough to do without waiting for an expression which might never come, enough to think about with all this getting up early. But she followed me upstairs, asking a dozen questions as to the hotel, the competition, the town, the food. These were nearly unanswerable. I had to invent something each time. And I needed to keep my wits keen to notice whatever might be unusual about the place. I needed to sniff and search. Because of the suitcase I had to pass the bedroom and go into the small dressing room. Madge bent down to begin unpacking, still talking. But I managed to interrupt:

–Just a moment, I must go out and see . . .

I left the little room and let my voice trail away. But Madge followed. I was near the bedroom door, felt her behind me, and even with my hand on the doorknob had to finish:

—. . . see whether the guelders are finished yet.

She caught quite lightly, but it seemed firmly, at my sleeve.

—You know you can see them better from the spare room. And anyhow, I can tell you they're finished, they'd fallen by the end of May.

So she had me back towards the dressing room and there again began to unpack. I stood over her, taking the hair brushes and the shoe horn and the Creamolin bottle, while she laid aside the clothes, while minutes ticked in the corners of the room. Presently she straightened up, a pair of shoes in her hands:

—Now you go and put these straight on the trees. I must just go a second.

I was left there alone with the shoes in my hand. I went over to the boot cupboard, already I was inserting the first smooth boxwood tree when it occurred that she might not have been going where I thought—she might have gone into the bedroom. I dropped the tree, and hurried out into the passage. I heard her moving in the bedroom. For a moment I hesitated. Even then I think I was conscious of my own dishonest motive, which was closer to me than even her possible guilt, and I hesitated. Then moved forward just as again she opened the door. Embarrassed, I began to whistle as I still walked forward. She stood there, wondering. I had almost to push past her into the doorway:

—Why, Henry, what do you want?

—What?

—Do you want anything?

—Can't I come into the bedroom if I wish?

She looked at me curiously.

—You needn't be so snappy. What's the matter?

I was already in the room and looking at the bed. I certainly had snapped at her—getting angry to help my own sense of shame. But now I lowered my voice, walking over to the blue silk armchair:

—Sorry. I suppose I'm just tired, didn't sleep much on the train. Wanted to sit down for a few minutes.

—Of course, darling, you just sit comfortable. I'll finish the suitcase.

She left me there. Why? Had she already had enough time to cover up things? Was she playing innocence, purposely leaving me alone to show she had nothing to hide? Why had she *rushed* into the bedroom? I looked round quickly. The bed was still unmade. Only one pillow was ruffled. The other lay smooth—but had she just smoothed it? I listened for her movements, the mutter of drawers opening and the whisper of clothes patted; she would be away some minutes, she always saw everything stowed in its proper place, she would rearrange clothes already misplaced in the drawers and cupboards. So I stood up, went to have another look at the bed, gave a quick turn back of the bedclothes. But no second hollow. Had she smoothed this away too? . . . Then over to the ash trays. I went round each of the three in the room, finally found some stubs in a blue glass cup near the dressing table. Madge smoked little, and always then with a cigarette holder—I knew her stubs, very small and perfectly dry, rounded: there were two of these—but the third was longer and chewed. I slipped this into my pocket. Examine it later. Next were the pots—to smell them for tobacco ash. Then the fireplace, the bed table. But nothing. I went to the curtains, curtains hold the odor of smoke. Nothing. Next

to the cushions, smelling these for a male hair oil or cream.
Again nothing— But did Diver wear hair oil? There were
still some seconds to go, I found myself stretching this
time period—I might have attributed to Madge the same
investigation as myself, imagining her to be going through
my things for some sign of a Liverpool street girl, contra-
ceptives or something. I stepped over quickly and was
looking under the bed—in books they often found socks
or something (though how a gentleman could forget his
sock?). But again saw nothing but deceptive eiderdown
feathers—each of which became a white pipe-cleaner until
I saw they were only those dry ridiculous feathers. I stood
up, looked round once more swiftly, alertly, efficiently—
then cursed myself for imagining that Madge would be
examining my things, she had never and would never do
such a thing.

—What are you looking for—burglars?

She was standing in the doorway, soundless on the
carpet:

—I thought you were tired and wanted to sit down?

She was looking at me closely indeed, her eyes that
were usually wide-open and astonished, now normal and
fixed with penetration, a nurse examining the sick. I felt
the awful red mounting in my cheeks, but just in time
thought:

—A stud. I've missed a stud for days.

How long had she been standing there? A stud would
cover everything, ash trays, fireplace, pots and all?

—A stud? Is that why you pick up cigarette ends and
put them in your pocket? Yes, your waistcoat pocket.
Give it here.

My hand had jerked protectively to the waistcoat as
she had spoken. So without saying a word I took it out

and handed it to her. I felt like a bad boy, toes turned in, dragging my arm forward—as boys accused move slowly and dogs crawl on their bellies. I was just going to explain that it was my absent mind, with the whiteness of the cigarette I had thought it a fresh one—when Madge, who had taken it from me, exclaimed slowly:

—But how curious, this isn't mine. I don't chew them like this.

She held the cigarette up between us, like a tiny spire of question, a piece in a game. She said, looking me straight in the eyes with strange persistence.

—Now who could have left this *here?* In my bedroom?

This was too provocative. As coldly, ironically, reservedly as I could, I said:

—That is exactly what *I* was wondering.

I looked down and then up quickly, as she said nothing. But Madge had been prevented from talking not by the expected sense of difficulty, or even of anger at such an exposure, but instead by a kind of radiance that spread throughout her face, that brought a soft light to her eyes, a rosiness to her cheeks, a smile of slow delight in the place of her wisely compressed lips of a moment before.

—Why, Hen! I do declare you think Maddie's had a gentleman friend! Hen!

For a terrible second I said nothing, simply stuttered. She was walking forward, her eyes alive, to embrace me.

—But isn't that sweet of him! Darling Hen, if you knew what a compliment that is, after all these years, Hen, to think Maddie's pretty enough for a gentleman friend. And Hen minds!

The bitch! I could only press her shoulders and stretch my mouth into the nameless laugh:

—Nonsense, Maddie—you're joking.

But she was convinced. And relishing the thought she
continued it:

—Now who could it be? The gardener? Old Pemberton
from over the road? I know, *I* know. Charley Diver!

—Nonsense! Really! Charley Diver, *that's* an idea!

The double bitch! The double-dealing, perfidious breed
of woman! I saw with nausea how cold-bloodedly arch she
could become. Her blue eyes shone, the blue bedspread
and a blue chair behind shone with the bedroom sheen.
She suddenly arched her neck back, held me at arm's
length, stared with a coy frowning smile into my eyes.

—D'you know, Henry-Penry—I've been thinking for
quite a time that you've been thinking that Charley's been
making up to me. Isn't that true? Own up, own up to
Maddie, now?

It was impossible to clench my fingers, I could not brace
myself physically in any way, I was too close. So in a
relaxed frame the lump in my throat rose like some lump
of pond slime, something bad struggling up under the
skin by the cord of my throat. And I could only say:

—Charley Diver? Charley? That's a good one! What a
kettle of fish that'd be! Charley Diver!

Madge's face puckered up into an expression of mock
admonition, she had finished playing this game, almost.
She still held the trump card:

—Well, Mister Detective, why didn't you look at the
windows?

I turned to the windows, half in response to her playing, but instinctively to see what she could mean. I saw
nothing.

—See how clean they are? Not a speck? Polished? Well,
Mister Holmes, the window cleaner was here yesterday and
something tells me he *might* have smoked a cigarette.

Then impatiently she went on:

—But really I don't know what things are coming to, window cleaners littering the place up with their ends; Enid not clearing the ash trays either. Everybody wants something for nothing these days.

Seeing her for a moment distracted, I began to talk again about Liverpool—this time I chose my own subject, the specific properties of Creamolin, a subject upon which I could freewheel without anxiety. To Madge's 'ums' and 'ahs' I went over Creamolin's consistency and ingredients, its perfume of old violets—not too cloying, sweet but fresh —its noninjurious effect on the sebaceous roots, the modernization of its bottle. I was wearing her down—finally without stopping I raised my voice and said jauntily:

—And now I'll be getting downstairs. A breather in the garden.

Before Madge, who was staring in the mirror and patting the back of her hair, had much time to object, I was out of the door and in the shadowed half-darkness of the landing passage. I breathed relief, a deflation of relief for such a scene ended, relief that I was out of that new shiny bedroom and in the sympathy of the friendly old landing. The mahogany banisters gleamed in the gray landing light, a large dark oil of some Scottish heath hung in shadow above the stair well, white cows shone out like patches of white plaster. Then suddenly I turned back along the passage and with my heart drumming—for it was a great risk after what had just happened—I went into Madge's bathroom, the pale-tiled place of plastic curtains, the light room smelling of water fresh like a swimming bath.

I went quickly over to the wash basin, bent over this and stared into the round black plug hole. Then, after a moment's pause, I dug my finger into the hole and dragged up what was there—a mass of hairs matted with wet gray soap. I smeared it flat on the clean white bowl. Closely, minutely, and listening with one ear towards the door, I inspected this smear. But what I was looking for was not there. Quickly I washed the smear away again into that plug hole—I had thought that perhaps if Diver had shaved there might be some bristles. Losing faith a little, I glanced round for perhaps a razor blade, perhaps the paper from a new blade, and I was walking out—when indeed I did catch sight of a blue crumpled-up ball of paper down on the floor in a corner. I paused, my pulses like ice; then, though not wishing it, I thought of Madge's armpits. Sometimes indeed she shaved . . . but who was to know when, or how often? This usually was done before an evening out in a sleeveless gown. Yet there were summer dresses without sleeves and it was June. I picked it up, stuffed it safely in that waistcoat pocket, and left the bathroom with long strides on tiptoe and hurried down the soft-carpeted stairs.

On the way to the garden I saw the door of the cupboard under the stairs. A dark-wood door topped with a machicolation of mahogany lurking like the wine cupboard it was. A sudden thought occurred, I took out my keys and opened the door. The beer was stored on a broad shelf running towards the wine nests—I knew exactly how many bottles were in, the order had been renewed only a few days before. But again a blank—all the bottles stood there, immaculate black clowns with white hats and ruffle labels, all in their precise row of dozen. I locked the door and walked along to the conservatory, and thence through to the garden.

My garden is some four times as long as it is broad.

At the end, at that time of year, a row of chestnuts screened with their heavy tropical leaves any vista of the houses beyond. Several smaller trees—laburnum, lilac, acacia—dotted the lengthy walls to either side. But in spite of the growth of rosebushes and others along the walls, in spite of the delphinium leaves already high and those of the other herbaceous plants—the walls still gave a rectangular sense to the garden, they gave at all times a sense of heavy shadow lined along their length. In the center ranges the oblong lawn—but halfway down this lawn there occurs a strange tumescence. A circular brick cylinder, like a small martello tower, rises almost in the center of the lawn—a trifle to one side of the exact center. The curved brick is creepered with wistaria, at that time in wistful bloom; and like a skirt to the tower there is set, in stony folds, a rising accumulation of marble and blue-gray rocks green with thick-leaved rock plants. To this promontory I walked—it was a place to which I would often walk with absent mind, an attracting pillar. I looked at the wistaria, not particularly thinking of it—then mounted a few little steps through the rocks, walked round the base of the tower and stood there thus hidden from the house.

Voices called from the next garden. From that small eminence I could see, over the ivied wall between us, Richard and Dicky cutting away at a weed patch with what looked like carving knives. At the sight of these, two of the inmates of Number 48, my interest quickened—it was impossible now for me to see any of my neighbors without imagining some propitious gift of information. Quietly, without knowing quite how to approach them, I watched. It was again a Saturday, possibly the two boys had the morning free. They seemed to be clearing a patch in the tall weeds that infested that end part of the next-door garden—a garden left wild from the back of Diver's yard wall. I watched for a while, and could only think that they must be clearing a space for some sort of court. A bundle of creosoted netting edged with white canvas lay to one side—perhaps this was going to be deck quoits.

The two boys were working hard, Dicky was stripped to the waist. As I watched the white young skin and the plying of its muscles I felt the air that breathed on such cool flesh, felt again in memory the supple freedom of my own youth, of the days of muscular play in the open air, beneath the sun, with the smell of grass and flowering trees fresher and stronger, deeper in the lungs than I had ever felt it since; the smell of bat oil, the hard feel of a new red cricket ball. Presently, and probably forced by those attentive eyes on his back, Dicky looked up, searched puzzled at the wall, and then must have seen me above it, a silent watcher at my tower of wistaria-ed brick. He looked for some time straight at me. Then, without calling a word, or waving, or making any gesture of recognition, he bent down again to his task. Only, a second later, I saw him mutter something to Richard, give a backward nod of his head in my direction—then go on cutting without again looking up. They were no more than fifteen yards away. It was a most pointed act of ignorance.

I stood there amazed. Only a week before I had been giving these two drinks at the Claverton, we had all laughed and talked together on the most amicable terms. And now?

I wondered what could have happened. I measured the distance again, looked for some obstruction between us, looked behind to see whether some more definite event beyond had overshadowed me, lastly looked down at my own person suspecting perhaps that some camouflage of wistaria had grown over my suit. But no—none of these —there must have been some other reason, perhaps they had mistaken me for the gardener or something—and the sun at least was behind me. I ventured to shout:

—Hello! What're you making? A tennis court?

Richard and Dicky stopped working, frozen it seemed by the sound of my voice, immobilized as they could only have been had they previously been sure I was there. They did not turn round immediately—but instead looked curiously at each other, debating whether or not to answer. Then Dicky turned his head, looked over to me, and shouted briefly:

—Deck tennis. All right with you?

He looked down again without smiling. I was astounded, then felt suddenly that this was my fault, I had committed some offense. I shouted that of course it was quite all right, a jolly good idea—before drawing back into my embarrassment. Then of course I remembered those moments on Diver's stairs, the figure of Bradford reflected in the windscreen, the disconcertment of Mrs. Lawlor, her intention to question Diver—all matters I had forgotten in the last hours of more instant trouble. Perhaps then Mrs. Lawlor had talked?

And they had begun to wonder at my behavior, I the only man at that time in the house? That would naturally have led to a common gossiping between everybody there. And just then, as if to confirm this possibility, a head poked out of a window—somewhere on the second floor— of the white-painted back of Number 48. I could not immediately see who this was, it was at most a woman with a scarf tied round her head in a dark low swathe, so that with her black hair hanging lank to either side she seemed to have the wild bob of a Mexican Indian. It was Mrs. Lawlor. She waved—and I waved back. But it was only a duster she had been waving—and now as she saw my arm greeting her, she too stopped as if horrified, and then with no answering gesture her head vanished—it was gone into the darkness of the room as if it had been sucked away by the force of her dissent.

I looked away, dared no longer look towards this house of sudden enmity, not risk the meeting of another pair of eyes. A cloud seemed to collect over my head. And this cloud then indeed became palpable, for just at that moment, as indeed frequently in my garden, a distant tremor seemed to shiver the earth, a rumbling came as from some eruption deep beneath the turf, and there blew up from the brick tower several wreaths of thick white smoke. The air thickened with a subterranean stench of burning minerals and for some seconds shadowed the light of the sun.

A goods train from the City had passed through the forlorn lightless tunnel deep beneath, throwing up smoke from the ancient right of its brick escape vent. This happened every so often in my garden, it happened just then. But I hardly noticed it, though ordinarily it was always an event for bitter and impotent disapproval. But now I had suddenly taken to myself, as jealous men do, a host of new enemies; a battery of fresh ridicule; a leveling of scorn that massed lips and eyes against me—me the lonely one, left by myself, out. I walked slowly back towards the house, ostensibly looking away from Number 48 to the other garden wall.

For the next half hour I sat in the little front morning room watching through one of the narrow gothic windows the drive of that house next door. Norma, I thought, might be going out for her Saturday shopping, it might be her free Saturday. She was the only one in the house who wanted something definite from me—she might be willing to tell me what was happening. Alone thus in the little-used shut-up room, a room old from lack of life, a room where once a half century before there had blazed a cheer-ful breakfast fire but which since had long lost the rustle of the morning paper and the white tablecloth and the smell of freshly cooked ham—thus alone I remember sit-ting, again watching unseen, again wondering whether I dared speak my mind, again deciding not to and then again taking fresh courage.

For once I was right. Norma soon did emerge to go smartly short-stepping down the steps next door. Quickly I grabbed up my hat and followed her down the street—pretending to be on my way to the shop in Seychelles Parade.

At first sight of me, when I sided up from behind her, she seemed to blink behind her spectacles, her face started. But Norma was not easily perturbed. That enamel seren-ity she had derived from some secret depths of the self-made girl's etiquette helped her now smile, pretend sur-prise, and say with the disarming attack which sometimes distinguished her suburbanity:

—Why, if it isn't Mr. Sykes!

—Mr. Sykes? I'm afraid . . .

—Oh, perhaps I've spoken out of my turn!

I managed a laugh. The pleasant discomfort of this girl's proximity, with its memories of our secret meeting and that disturbing dance, returned with full conflicting force; the almost empty avenue along which we were walking seemed to fill with people and eyes, people where the tree trunks lined the curb and eyes in every window. Yet I was determined to persevere: this girl was the key to much, already the reference to Sykes drew uneasily near to my suspicions. So I managed a joking tone, but at the same time shot her a glance of conspiracy above my own lowered spectacles. Our two eyes met thus in glances from above the armor of glasses, she from the side, mine over the top. It must have been rather like two lispers talking together—but more painful, more secretive, for those glasses were true armor.

—Why, Miss Devereux—Norma! Cards on the table! Were you referring by any chance to a Mr. Bill Sykes?

—Well, I wouldn't say I wasn't, in a manner of speaking.

—Mr. Sykes, if my memory holds good, was a character of crime. And what a coincidence, now that you should mention him—the last time I heard of a burglar mentioned was in your very own house! By Mrs. Lawlor, it was. She thought Charley Diver was a burglar. When he came back that evening he went to his Old Boy's Dinner.

—Well now, isn't it funny you should say that! There's been talk about that night.

—Talk?

—Charley says he never came back.

—Never? How could he say that? I'd swear I— I seem to remember chatting with him for a second. Sounds funny to me—

—To tell the truth, Mr. Bishop, that's what a lot of people thought. Funny. No offense meant.

A pause. We looked at each other wisely. Then I chose to continue in the same tone—although we were only two it seemed better to drape this difficult discussion with a diplomatic severity, another sort of armor:

—I was going to ask you, Miss Devereux, your opinion on another matter. I had the impression this morning that one or two of your friends in Number 48 showed

towards me an attitude I might describe as 'cool.' Now
I wonder why that could be, could I have been mistaken?

—I'm sure you must have made a mistake, I'm sure I
don't know.

—By the way, how's the hair style? Do you think of
coming along again? I could arrange it quite easily. . . .

—Now, Mr. Bishop, that *is* kind of you. It'd be lovely
to come next week—of course, I'd have to find out from
the manager when.

—Just let me know. At the same shop, you know.

—I know the one.

—That's fixed then. Now what were we saying—yes,
wasn't it funny how I got the impression of a certain
coolness? I thought living in the house you might know.
Now come on, we're friends, aren't we?

—Well . . . if you do really want to know—

—I'd be *grateful*, Miss Devereux.

And then the cat was out of the bag. Norma opened
her mouth and the story came out complete, as though
no brain thought the words but the lips alone worked:
though I suppose it was the opposite—women usually do
not speak, they think with their lips:

—It's really all about that evening and Charley Diver
there's been talk it's funny Mrs. Lawlor says that you
were the only man in the house and you said you spoke
to Charley and Charley swears he never came back and
they say that if the man had been a burglar then he would
have taken something only as it was the drawers had been
opened and nothing gone. Mrs. Lawlor says you were
such a time gone she began to wonder what you were doing
such a long time away plenty of time she says to go
creeping about the passages, up and down the stairs she
says it's the quiet ones that make the dark horses and she's

heard that your maid Enid told her girls that you go
away some nights and stay away. What does he do away,
Mrs. Lawlor asks? What does he bring back in that suitcase? Of course I laugh you know me Mr. Bishop but you
know what tongues are everybody getting their heads
together in the house. And hey presto you're a gentleman
burglar! Now I think that's too silly I call it disgraceful
if you ask me what I think . . .

And so on it went, she simply kept on talking, saying
in fact all she thought, raising her voice in a crusade
against gossip and in eulogy of my own reputation. I
stopped listening, my mind just revolved what I had just
heard. Surprisingly, the cloud lifted as the facts were
made certain. Now I knew exactly what must be faced.
Patently the campaign with the people at Number 48
had suffered a decisive reverse—the affair called for instant action, action of some kind as violent as theirs.
I had to think seriously. I walked on with Norma to the
end of the avenue—she talked all the time—and then, to
think more clearly, to avoid further risk of Madge's mood,
and indeed to avoid the whole area of conflict, went to sit
in my shop alone.


That evening at dinner—a cold dinner in a summer-
cold dining room, with the June evening's light grayed by
cloud, and darkened further by the dusky yellow of a
shaded still electric light—I said to my wife:

—I've been thinking—what you said was right.

Madge, whose eyes had been dreaming distantly with
the end of the white tablecloth and the gray-soaped evening beyond the windows, started and frowned:

—I said I *knew* hydrangeas plant easily now.

—Yes, dear. I mean, what you said the other day about

me . . . not taking too much interest in things, not being my old self.

—Oh.

—I've been thinking perhaps we aren't getting round enough these days.

—Speak for yourself, dear.

—Mm?

—But, Henry, didn't you say it was business troubling you?

—So it was, is. But that's no reason not to take ourselves out of ourselves now and then. I think we don't *do* enough. Why don't we have a real outing, like we used to?

—Outing? Why, only . . .

—I mean a real one. What about the river? Remember how we used to go down with quite a crowd, have a picnic, spend the day?

—Ten years ago at least.

But Madge was already smiling, her eyes I saw were away with memories of old days, summer scenes that seemed all sunlight and warmth, willow tracings on the slow water, the smell of varnished boats, the shrimp-paste sandwiches wrapped in their lace paper. Redolence of weeds, hands drifting in cool water—they drifted almost across her face. Men in white flannels, a wide summer hat shading her eyes to shine more brilliant in the feminine dusk. She turned to me with some excitement:

—What do you really mean?

—Well, why don't we make up a party? And go—take some punts out?

—But, Henry, everybody's so scattered, the old crowd, we could never get them.

Then I pretended to be thinking. I nodded reminiscently at her mention of 'the old crowd.' And for a moment then

indeed I found myself not pretending, distracted by the
memory of those old friends, and of the days when our
own time together had been younger. In spite of my
present intention, I did feel a physical inward softening,
I glanced up at my wife and saw her with what suddenly
was overwhelming love; but it was a love of yearning,
for already it seemed she was removed, that she had once
been mine but could be no more—though during that
second I had to fight with a most urgent desire to ask
her back to me on any terms, to plead humbly—and to
confess above all my machinations. But the wish faded,
the worm of hurt pride caught at me, and I said:

—Look, Madge—what about asking the people next
door along?

I saw in her eyes a sudden surprise, and knew that surprise in her was often followed by disapproval, by a need
to condemn any new matters not in their accustomed
place. So I went on quickly:

—After all, we've been seeing a bit of them lately—and
you seem to find them a jolly lot. I like the boys, old Mrs.
Lawlor isn't a bad sort. There's Bradford, he's an interesting fellow, and Charley'll always make a party go—
shouldn't be surprised if he wouldn't manage a car too.
That's an idea—these chaps in garages often have a car
on their hands. We could make up a picnic lunch here,
and I'd stand Sam for the boats—

—But, Henry, isn't it all rather expensive?

—Boats? No. We could start at Shiplake, or even
Goring. Remember Goring?

—Do you think we really *know* them well enough for
this?

I kept my eyes fixedly away while I replied:

—We knew some better than others, certainly.

Madge showed no sign of emotion. I persevered and played my trump:

—Still, if you think it unwise . . .

Her immediate objection had been registered; she had my agreement to withdraw the idea, she was won. I am sure she was already imagining the effect this or that food might produce, whether the second-best table linen would impress sufficiently, what dress to wear. It was safe to back her up:

—Well, why not? At least there's nothing to lose—why don't *you* go across this evening and ask them?

—Me?

—It'd be more informal coming from you, just drop in.

—Of course Mrs. Lawlor would be the one to ask.

—Let's make it soon, while the weather holds? A Sunday naturally, say next Sunday?

She was already looking at her plate, she saw that she had finished. Now animated she rose:

—I'll slip across right away. I'll ask her what she thinks.

—No, dear, make it an invitation, a definite invitation.

She was already near the door:

—And, Madge, if you think it sounds a bit ostentatious, if *you* think so, tell them I've been away making arrangements for the renovating of the shop, and that this is a little celebration. Eh?

Not until she was out of the front door did I see and regret this last mistake. It might easily decide them that I had 'made a bit' on my nights away! It was ridiculous of course. But still all I could do was shrug my shoulders.

She came back half an hour later.

—It's all settled. Sunday. I saw Charley, and he was most enthusiastic, said he'd beat up the gang. Though I must say they seemed a bit funny at first, almost stand-offish. I suppose it was the suddenness.

# 6

Our two cars drove in erratic convoy down a wide concrete road leading west and to the river. Erratically—for
the first car, driven by Charley Diver, always outdistanced
the second, whose wheel was held by Richard Dawk.
Charley on a borrowed accelerator could not resist showing off—whenever possible he spurted ahead and out of
sight.

Bradford next to me in the rear seat would lean forward and tap him on the shoulder, exclaiming always with
a novel urgency that he could no longer see the 'others.'
Madge sitting beside Diver hoped that they had not lost
their way. And so the car was slowed until in the distance
the silver bonnet and Richard's striped blazer would be
seen approaching at speed from the anxious road back.
Then Charley pressed the accelerator again and the convoy would be off to repeat the same process. Discussion
of the right road to take never stopped. Charley assured
us he knew the way. Madge carried on her knee a map she
found difficulty in reading and so ceaselessly queried the
direction. Bradford, who had often driven to the same
river town from a different direction and on a not dis-
similar road, thought at times he was on the same road

and interrupted the two in front with his added misdirec-
tion. I had no opinion to offer; on the other hand I was
the host, I was in charge of affairs, so now and then I
forced myself to add a suggestion that further compli-
cated our progress.

Thus consistently anxious we sped on our way west,
along the great new concrete roads, through blind rows
of small red houses, under new concrete bridges, past
hoardings and unknown settlements sprouting suddenly
their shops round liner-like cinemas, past factories of
concrete built like strange diving boards or running as
ceaseless sheds that seemed to race along beside us, past
patches of field and tree that at first promised the beginning of the country but an instant later disappeared in
a reiteration of arterial brick, past eccentric groups of
older houses standing alone like weathered ghosts—until
at last the town fell off, and with a dwindling of slice-like
rogue houses the hedges and hutments and dwellings of
the country began. Thick green banked the sides of a
secondary road into which we turned, the elder flower
blossomed everywhere like a warm scattering of snow.
Through villages we drove—strange places that began as
suddenly as they ended, leaving no distinct pattern of
their being except surprise—until at last the river drew
near. We entered low-lying fields that smelled of moisture:
here already the houses took on boatworthy trappings
—white wood balconies, verandas walled with planking,
carved eaves and flagpoles; there were boats, old bottom-
up boats, in the gardens.

We drew into the town and braked at the river's edge
in front of a small hotel. One could see the ranks of
moored boats nosing the landing stage like fine-varnished
chrysalids. Then Charley, Madge, Bradford and I sat for

a moment waiting in the car, all heads turned to the road, tense in the last anxiety that the other car would have missed the way. But bringing much relief it came bustling round the corner, anxious faces peering from it, and then spurted up alongside. Out came Mrs. Lawlor, Dicky, Richard, and a girl these two had brought called Craig. We greeted each other as two safari parties at some perilous destination—and then began the unloading of wicker picnic baskets, the search for the thermos flask, the unshipment of strange tartan rugs, the assurances of what a fine day this was.

A fine, sun-high day in June. It was already nearly twelve, the sky above a deep blue. There was a high wind, odd for such a clear warm day, and it gave the sun an added fierceness; I remember an impression that a few fields away, or round the next bend of the river, there might have been a tract of desert breeding such a great draft. The boats rocked and creaked as the wind caught them; across the river a chestnut shone silver, its leaves all blown back like rabbit's ears. The surface of the slow water itself was rough with ripples. There was a feeling of the sea, a sailing dinghy came racing down before the wind at a speed foreign to the river; precipitously heeling, it arrived, passed, disappeared like a small butterfly round a lower bend of the reach.

I remember looking at this passing boat with pleasure, feeling the invigoration of the wind and sunlight. I led the party down to the boats, listened to the pleasant gurgling beneath the wood planks. On that perceptibly springy and nautical landing stage I felt an able feeling, a stirring to be on the water, and a capable boatworthy sense of knowledge. I was determined to impress. I sur-

veyed the boats professionally, ignoring the punts, and
ordered from the boatman two skiffs.

The others were coming down the steps in single file,
carrying baskets and rugs and sunshades; the boatman
wandered about impassively providing oars and a variety
of flowered cushions. It had been agreed to row a mile
or so upriver to an area of backwaters which would pro-
vide shade and seclusion for lunch. I set about placing my
guests. It was important that Diver should go into the
first boat with Madge.

—Dicky, how about you going in first with Charley?
And as for feminine ballast—Madge, I think. Mrs. Law-
lor's coming with me in the second, aren't you, Mrs.
Lawlor?

—Oh, but, Mr. Bishop, don't you and your wife . . . ?

—Nonsense, we see quite enough of each other as it is,
don't we, dear?

I followed this firmly by taking her arm and helping
Madge into the unsteadiness of the first boat.

After much swaying to our various seats, we started
off. In the first boat Dicky and Diver at the oars, with
Madge steering and the girl Craig wedged like a trousered
figurehead in the bows. In the second boat Richard Dawk
pulling in front, Bradford on the other oar, and Mrs.
Lawlor and myself together on the rudder seat. We went
in single file. The lengths between the two boats gradually
increased, with Bradford insisting on a leisurely pull in
view of his age, his stomach, and the sabbatical natural
of the day.

They talked picnic talk—facetious, high-spirited in a
holiday mood. I was concentrated on the boat up in front;
I just remember odd remarks—once about Norma.

Dark Richard shouted from the front of the boat:

—Pity she couldn't get here, a lot more use on an oar than the illustrious L. H.

Bradford grunted back:

—You ought to have had that strong young Craig of yours in this one. I'll bet she'll be taking over from Charley soon.

—Can't keep a good girl down.

Then Mrs. Lawlor said to me in a tone of severe surprise:

—Did you say Norma was working today, Mr. Bishop? Working?

—Mm? Yes, yes indeed, a Sunday on or something.

—Still, she's coming down to the Crown for supper I heard? Seems she can get off early enough for *that*, seems she can fix *that* all right.

I was hardly listening. With my hand on the tiller I had to crane sideways to keep the forward boat in view. But the possibility of the girl Craig taking over from Diver was interesting—Diver would have to sit in the back with Madge. And sure enough exactly this was happening. The other boat was swinging in midstream, Craig's figure could be seen edging over Dicky bent sideways bowed over his waiting oar. The boat rocked. I could see Diver standing unsteadily upright and reaching forward to clutch the back seat where Madge was sitting. As our boat came nearer, so the figures grew larger, more discernible—and it was suddenly clear that neither Craig nor Diver wore trousers! In that short time they had taken the opportunity to wriggle from their trousers and emerge riverwise in the bathing trunks they must have worn beneath. So now they were settled, Madge and half-naked Diver, arm against arm on the tiller-seat cushions;

the boat was swung round again, and Dicky and Craig began to row with new energy.

Although for a purpose I had precipitated these conditions, I could not help feeling anxious—most anxious that the other boat should be kept in sight so that at least I could see whatever might happen. And so I began, at first casually, but growing impatient, to exhort Bradford to 'put a bit more muscle to it.' Still—I could not go too far. Bradford might have offered me the oar—and then I should have seen nothing. So, carefully exhorting, painfully cracking a joke with dark Richard and the time of day with Mrs. Lawlor, I steered up that anxious river.

It was almost empty, it was a reach far up and not too many boats were about. I remember that once there came chugging along like some cremation barge a small pleasure steamer, white and low-funneled, with glass observation windows, and a closely packed crowd of merrymakers forward, gazing like dead bees. To a distant popular song this passed, and again the river was empty. Our boats thus held the center stream, and alone in file they began to feel like two Viking craft coursing the inlets. Oars like long flies' legs rose and fell to either side of the forward boat, the sun high beyond blackened their silhouette against the silver water. And still that wind blew, clean, warm, fierce. To either side the long riverside grasses on their flat meadows weighed back against this mineral draft. Though chestnuts flapped back their lopping leaves like ears, an acacia wove its delicacies like yellow weed in a tidal crevice, and willows by the water swam in the air drowned. Leaning grasses stood topped with green feathers; now and then sporadic fogs of seed rose like a river mist above them. That wind blew high, tanning the sunshine, a horizontal wind, a flag tautener, a wind that dazed the summer day. And up high above, to reinforce such a booming wraith, the sky redoubled its blue, reinforced itself to royal heliotrope, deep, deep blue of vertiginous depth.

Dazzled and ruffled by so much light and wind, I squinted to peer forward and once it seemed that Diver's arm was around Madge, that their heads lay close together. The boat was far off now, it was more than ever difficult to be certain. And such uncertainty I could not endure—I got up and stood swaying with hands outstretched to Bradford. Instantly—I did not have to say a word—Bradford was up and moving towards me, for a moment we stood thus face to face like two people blocking each other's path in the street, and then passed clinging to one another's shoulders. The boat slid on, but lost speed. With a thump I sat down on that hard seat, and began to pull heartily. The boat swung round, Richard was taken unawares; and now as the boat gathered speed they began to shout their delight, with which I joined as much as I could:

—What ho, she bumps!

—A life on the ocean wave!

—One! Two! Three! *And* four! That's the stuff, boys, just keep it steady, just like that.

Bradford had settled comfortably against Mrs. Lawlor, who had lost some of her wistfulness and had begun, quietly and turning her head away, to giggle at the hilarities which now for some time accompanied each stroke. I pulled forcefully—the rowlocks clanked and the boat shuddered at every forward surge, Richard was delighted, athletically soon silent. We feathered the water with our backward stroke, bringing with this a sense of strong ease. But such apparent ease concealed a withering cloud in the back of my head, the itching back of a head with no eyes wondering what was happening beyond, wondering whether the distance between the boats had decreased. And to add to these anxieties, I could see now Bradford's right arm was already round Mrs. Lawlor, it was the natural position for an arm when two people sat on such a narrow seat. But what more intimate?

Soon my hands were smarting, and my breath short. A slow sweat like tears of anger clouded my eyes. Meanwhile Bradford was droning to the boat at large, and to the narrow sky:

—Ghosts of Henley, gallant gentlemen and fair ladies on the lawns of Phyllis Court. Tea and strawberries, strawberries and cream, cream and salmon, salmon and parasols, parasols and picture hats, cucumber and the clink of hock! The marine band extolled on plaintive trumpets Land of Hope and Glory, Galsworthy stood under the white trellised arches of the clubhouse, against the green shone the white laces of the ladies, the flannels of the gentlemen, the white vests of passing oarsmen. Violet eyes in the shade of a parasol, old oarsmen in pink livery, shades of the sunblind and the red geranium, hydrangeas blue in their white urns . . . and far away the mounting clouds as in Berlin the war lord on his saddle seat dreamed the vengeance of a withered arm. . . .

So he droned on, this yellow-toothed Bradford leaning back carious in the sunlight, while at such an evocation of past summers Mrs. Lawlor in her striped summer dress grew again wistful.

And then it was as if Bradford had invoked the very wrath of the war lord—for over from the east now came mounting a vast pile of cloud. Then suddenly the empty river seemed full of boats, all in a flash, a shocking looming of boats—yet it was only one, the boat with Madge

and Charley on, which suddenly appeared alongside to
the surprised corners of our eyes; they had been drifting
downstream for some time, they had already seen those
ominous clouds. A scream came:

—Ahoy there!

It was not the scream that made me nearly drop my
oar. It was Diver's arm round Madge and plainly cuddling
her as she laughed. And his great white red-haired knee
very near her leg, which in the low seat itself showed an
inch of peach-colored bloomer. Richard shouted:

—Oho, look at the lovebirds!

I blushed dark with shame. I smiled sick joy and tried
to look at Dicky Carter. But one eye—it felt like a wall
eye—was tied by its muscle to those two in the back seat.
A boiling disgust, a positive sad nausea at the sight of
those two together in the flesh tore at me savagely; gone
altogether was the wish to provoke some certain gesture
of this sort. I only managed to scan the clouds with a
nautical eye and shout:

—Dirty weather ahead!

Richard called to Dicky:

—Make fast to the bank, eh?

Diver chose at that moment to yell in mock terror to
Madge:

—Heavens, your husband! For God's sake . . .

And made a great fuss of disengaging his arm from
round Madge's neck, lurching over to one side of the boat,
pressing himself away from Madge and bellowing with
laughter at himself. Very nearly he upset the boat at this,
which brought all eyes round to share the joke. Everybody
laughed. I remember very clearly that no more could be
seen of Diver than his thick red throat—his face was
thrown back and laughing to the sky. But Madge's eye

I caught—I saw it with a nervous photographic clarity—
I saw her glance sharply at me. I knew instantly that she
had remembered our talk of Diver a few nights before;
and that she was conscious of this situation—if it had
been altogether a joke then such a look would never have
come to her face? And if in the first place Diver had put
his arm round her purely for comfort, then the joke itself
would never have been made? The laughter subsided and
eyes turned again to the sky. But I remembered with curious fixity those two pictures—Madge's suddenly sharp
and humorless eyes, and Diver's bare upturned throat, a
fat red fowl's neck.

As we drifted, there appeared a square-cut breach in
the bank, a sheltered canal water; black and unmoving,
it disappeared in a sharp turn of its gardened bank. The
garden looked wild, roses straggled like wild thorn; the
roof of a crumbled boathouse jutted its logged boat
planking above the roses. Such a creek looked sheltered—
we turned towards it. The clouds had reached the sun,
turning the water gray-green as now the first few rain-
drops came coining the water.

For a while, perhaps overcome by the sudden shadow
across the day, perhaps by a new windless calm, perhaps
by the dark strangeness of the creek itself, no one spoke.
No room for oars to stretch wide, we paddled quietly in
this darker water; sudden solitary noises, a grinding rowlock, a wooden creak sounding uncomfortably loud and
dangerous in the new enveloping quiet. Now too the heavy
smells of wet vegetation, of mud-soaked roots hung thickly
and forlornly about; yet thickly too, and with a beautiful
wildness, the roses grew above, white roses like scattered
paper over their high dense bushes. We rounded a bend
and the boathouse came into view. It looked deserted. By

its side, even more derelict, streaked and weathered with disuse, lay moored a sad blue-painted houseboat, its windows smashed, its kitchen funnel grate-brown with rust. The hedges to either side rose high, the red chimney of a house could be seen it seemed sleeping above the roses—but it was hedged remote, it was far from the isolation of the boathouse and the houseboat. The rain began to fall quicker. With some misgiving the first boat turned and entered the dark tunnel of the boathouse. The second followed, slipping quietly against the landing stage.

They had all begun talking again, all at once choosing or denying this houseboat, veering and naggling for houseboat or boathouse—but now in the tunnel their voices echoed woodenly, as if some amplifier had been switched on them by the hidden owner, as if their voices were not themselves but those of a sudden crowd outside and on the roof and all around. For a second everyone stopped silent and listened—then as immediately burst into loud laughter. Any misgivings that they were trespassing seemed instantly to be dispersed; the two boys leaped with agility onto the rotting wood landing stages, Bradford began to suspect in a loud and pleased voice the presence of water rats, Diver pretended to squeal like a girl and to lift his absent skirts, Madge fussed for the picnic baskets, Craig who spoke little helped Richard and Dicky make the boats fast. I felt myself for some seconds still nervous that we might be doing wrong—and then I noticed also that Mrs. Lawlor looked apprehensive too: we, of course, were the only two habitual property owners. However, as the rain outside settled into a sheet across the open doorway, it was easy for me to formulate to myself unspoken excuses for shelter. I helped unload the picnic baskets—anything to occupy myself, to take my mind off the vision of those two in the back seat, to re-establish myself as host. I think I began to chant out names of the sandwich packets: fish paste, meat paste, egg and cress, cress and cucumber, liver sausage, and Real Lobster. I forced myself to shout to Diver:

—Ah, we've caught a crab, I see!

Somebody tittered but nobody much laughed. They were all too busy. While Madge and Mrs. Lawlor set the picnic cloth and the food out on two of the boat seats, most of the others were bemoaning the bad luck of such weather—standing transfixed in the gateway and looking helplessly at the rain; and then examining with some excitement the watery wood and varnished shelves of our refuge. I too examined it—I remember it, and much else of that afternoon's scene very clearly, for I was nervous, upset, and my eyes were constantly looking at things to avoid meeting the eyes of people.

Though it had looked rotten from outside the roof was sound. From its tall vault there hung an heirloom of giant cobwebs like black rigging—together with the real but rotted rigging and ropes of small sailing craft; on a high rack the varnished keel of a dinghy glinted dully through dust and a pale smear of lichen; Richard and Dicky measured this up and gave it some technical name, while Craig their camp follower nodded wisely—they all three stood with arms akimbo looking up with an oddly serious air of ownership. On shelves round the walls other derelictions of the river—half-empty jars of varnish caked dry that reminded me of butterfly-killer jars; creosote tins; a drum of tar; a pile of old sailcloth that Diver picked up for use as a tablecloth—only to grab away a rotten shred busy with insect eggs, pale spiders, blind-white millipedes. Coils of small rope, a long boat hook, three paddles whose ancient varnish had turned black; on the rack long wooden punting poles, automatic hooks, bunting, camp stools, a cheap faded Union Jack. This last Diver again pounced on—and with assumed severity laid it across one of the boat seats as a cloth. Without hesitation Mrs. Lawlor, in memory of past wars and sacrifices, boldly told him he ought to be ashamed of himself. Charley removed it with facetious gestures of ceremony that did little to hide an awkward moment.

It may have been the rain that provoked this and many other small awkwardnesses that thereafter bit like gnats into the cheerfulness of the afternoon. For the rain had settled in to fall steadily, sheeting the black water with silver, curtaining with threadlike jets the doorway, drumming on the wooden roof, dribbling a mercurial slobber over a single small windowpane high up near the roof. In the double damp of the new fresh water pouring outside and the breeding black water that gurgled under our feet, we sat and ate our sandwiches, pulled apart the small lobsters, drank the beer and lemonade I had provided. The landing stages were dusty, we had to remain in the two boats, half clustered round the food, half sitting on the narrow seats and mostly facing in one direction like riders in some dismal, flood-locked tram. An air of false twilight, a dark wet gloom spawned on the constricted air.

However, at first a popping of corks and a cracking of jokes, cries of outraged joy and little shrieks of wonder, titterings and antics and with them the sudden rain-filled silences—sounds of the sun parlor on rainy seaside afternoons. Charley Diver tried to occupy the breach, certain that he was the life of the party. As though it had all been arranged he produced a pack of cards and did

many card tricks. He told fortunes. He cut the cards
and brandished them with prestidigitous fluttering. He
was assisted by Bradford—who in an attitude of disgusted
superiority behaved like the serious half of a cross-talk
duet. All was grist to Charley's delighted mill, and so
was Madge's bright laughter and applause. I pretended
to take an amazed interest in the tricks—but my eyes
kept returning to Charley's bare knees. Surely he might
have put his trousers on to eat? Mrs. Lawlor, mellowed
by a little beer, sat primly against the wicker end seat
and nodded her approval; she was filled with the most
delicate parts of the lobsters, but still smiled wistfully—
as if, though she had perhaps consumed more of the en-
joyable things than anyone else, enjoyment could never
be hers. Dicky, Richard, and Craig, the youngest in the
party, remained curiously the most silent, the least ex-
hilarated. The reason, I think, was Craig. Both the boys
must have felt some attachment to her, but neither admitted it—they would both have been the kind that
inherits well into manhood the schoolday conception that
girls are 'soft stuff' and no companion for serious sporting men: 'stag' parties, plenty of beer—'religion and
politics' barred from the conversation. However, with
Craig they made a concession—she was a handsome but
not pretty type of sporting girl who said little, looked
seriously impassive and frankly insensitive, an adult tom-
boy of pleasing appearance whose limbs were clean and
showed no perfumed guile. So that of all the party now
these three sat together and, frowning, talked together
of serious things, of the bowlings and the battings of the
world.

After his card tricks, Charley with undiminished energy
showed us the hornpipe up and down the creaking landing

stage, his large figure prancing huge above us, his bare feet setting awkwardly—like naked male feet on a shingle beach—as palely they hopped. All the time splitting his ginger mustache with great bellows of laughter, he found two tent pegs and a dried paintbrush with which he juggled. He put his hands together and made the noise of a mouse near Mrs. Lawlor, he took out a penny which instantly disappeared only to be dragged the next moment from behind Madge's ear. Since Madge's shrill laugh infected him, he proceeded to draw more pennies from Madge—it seemed to me for a particularly long time. Then he went too far—extracted one of the pennies from her arm-pit.

—Why, she's the girl of my dreams, she's full of money!

—Charley! Don't! You make me feel like the Bank of England.

—The Old Lady of Threadneedle Street herself!

—*Thank* you, Mr. Bradford.

—Granted.

This sort of thing was infectious. Now Bradford suddenly yelled:

—Oi! There she goes, there she goes . . . !

—Who?

—Where?

—What?

—A fine fat beauty! A rat!

—Oh!

—Help!

—All alive-oh, big as a cat, black, wet, and slippy.

—Ugh.

—Don't worry, Mrs. Bishop, there'll be another along shortly. They hunt in herds.

In fact a large water rat had slipped suddenly from

under the water end of the landing stage and swiftly, drawing its straight cord of a tail, had swum to the opposite bank, vanishing into the overhanging grass. The little raised head and its submerged body had made no sound at all; but Bradford had seen it with delight.

—Whatever next, sewer rats indeed, and I thought this was a *nice* part of the river.

—*Not* sewer rats, Mrs. Lawlor. Water rats, voles in fact. As Mrs. Bishop knows, they infest the banks in hordes, their tails are often fifteen inches long. Did you see its teeth? Great burrowers, voles, great burrowers.

—Oh, do be quiet, Mr. Bradford.

Dicky Carter's low pink forehead was ridged with horizontal lines, thinking; dark Richard frowned and eased his jaw; Craig stared at the water serene and blank, expressionless and ruffled by no vole. Richard said deeply:

—Used to see them out with the otter hounds. Ever run, Craig?

—Can't say I have.

I had to say something. I had to keep established my position as host. I remember then trying to quote something I had read in the encyclopaedia:

—Know what they feed on? Fish, small fish. But the interesting thing is that they make nests out of the bones of their food, regular water rats' nests. . . .

But then I trailed off, for although for once at this astonishing news several faces stared in my direction— I knew that as usual I had mixed up things. I was thinking of something else, of a river bird, indeed of a kingfisher. I pressed my lips, furious at such inaccuracy, decided not to correct it and instantly felt a sense of duplicity. So I reached for the aluminum head of the thermos flask and mumbled:

—Anyone ready for a cup of tea?

Of course they were. The incidence of tea again stimulated the talk. They relapsed, in relief after that scared hiatus, into jokes, more wild cheeriness. It went on until tea was finished, and there was nothing left but the rain. Even Diver then quietened, he sat down moodily and perhaps exhausted on one of the boat seats and with one finger began to twiddle round a rowlock. At each turn it gave a regular, grating, tired squeak.

And the rain poured on down. Not in one incessant sheet—it varied, nearly stopped and then with a different rhythm began again. I remember the hours of staring at it. How many different ways it can rain! One felt on that afternoon that it tried every variation of its wet repertoire. With the violence of its first cloud, it had broken in deluge, knifing down quite vertically its curtain, screening the air with watered silver wire. That first violence had abated, a small wind had carried the lighter wider lines of rain to a slant—the surface of the river had resolved its silver coinage into a sluggish mirror just flecked by light strokes as at the passage of a fleet of water insects. Suddenly the lightening sky had grown purple dark again, a sulphurous yellow radiance had traveled at speed from the east, and without warning, and only for the space of some three minutes, the air had been white with a rain of hailstones. Some of these collected like crumbled soda on the projecting ends of the landing stage; though white they fell like a storm of heavy soot against the shining brass sky; they made a cruel whipping sound, danced like mad white peas. Yet soon—as at the command of the human agency that seems to control storms—this temper had exhausted itself; and for a while in a sullen windless air the rain had showered into lighter, finer drops of the texture of mist, of a most penetrating damp. A bloom of wetness had then moistened the inside of the boathouse, a sweat suffused clothes, hands, wood with its clammy dew. And how low the clouds had hung then, an accumulated grayness of damp mist rolling within its thickness and hanging, always hanging down and over. The trees no longer rustled to the lively drops—a clean sound like the refreshment of birds—but now dropped dogged and wet, miserable and drenched, stifled with too much water: no tree could breathe in such dense moisture.

Disconsolate, with tea done, the party resorted much to its own individual resources. There were long silences, silences that admitted openly how everyone wished now they had never come. Boredom became petulance, almost anger—which I should think was exacerbated by the lack of any scapegoat; no one could be blamed. No one had now the grace to exert themselves—and so Craig and the boys were bent over some fictitious game, Mrs. Lawlor had brought out a small half-made purse and her crochet hooks, Bradford and Madge and I played a game of cards. Only Diver did nothing but sit on his seat. I watched him over the cards, saw him once or twice open his mouth, look at the engaged company, then shut it, staring again moodily at the river. Once I caught him looking at Madge, concentratedly. It occurred to me that he was frustrated by this enforced sheltering—I grew disturbed as I imagined in detail how he had planned to spend much of the day with Madge, scheming to be alone with her, to charm her away from the party for a stroll or something. My mind kept returning to the sight of him and Madge on that boat's back seat—I remembered so well the legs, that upturned neck, Madge's peculiar look. In a way I became

the only one contented with the rain. I thanked the heavens
for the water that kept them in.

But at six o'clock the clouds grew bright, the pale
white sun fired their wool with warm strong light. The
rain dithered away to nothing. The sun came through,
and one by one and then suddenly as if in a chorus the
birds came squawking and trilling out. The gnats rose.
Everything glistened into evening gold. A dog barked;
and across the early evening water came the distant, infi-
nitely melancholy strains of a music-hall song played on
a summer gramophone. Windows everywhere must have
been opened. Lungs must have greeted the new air, eyes
turned pleased to the sky.

With all that time to spare, none of us had thought
of packing up—so that now the boathouse echoed the
scramble of packing, cries again and laughter and delighted grunts, all the epidemic excitement of freedom.
We pushed off, and in gondola file paddled silently through
the narrow water towards the river. Charley's spirits had
risen to the weather with animal violence, and now as he
saw that old blue houseboat with its diving board decks,
he almost upset his boat by suddenly standing up, gripping his shirt as if to fling it off, and shouting:

–Who's for a bathe? Race any comer to the Skylark!

But for once his buoyancy met with immediate disapproval.

–Can it! You'll have the boat over.

–Siddown.

For a second—a delightful second to me—Charley
swayed confusedly on bent naked legs. His mustache
seemed to split uncertain into two halves as his mouth fell
open—and then he gave his shoulders a shrug. But even

before he had sat down again the old smile was gathering
and he was able to wail in a deep, mock-injured tone:

—Can't a fellow drown himself in peace nowadays?

Bradford called dryly from our boat:

—With the *greatest* of pleasure. If it's a thorough job.

—I promise you it will be. *I'm* going to drown the *inner*
man.

At which there was a great burst of laughter. Charley
joined loudly, adding uproariously: 'With a gallon of the
Best.' He was on top again. As always, a mention of beer
had broken down all defenses, it was never mentioned without a feeling of conspiratorial delight. Charley knew it,
and back he was in everyone's esteem.

Except mine—now he was back near Madge in the first
boat. True he was now again rowing, but even this was
bad; Diver rowed face to face with Madge and all manner
of intimate glances could be exchanged. And there was
the question of his half-naked body moving only a few
feet from Madge's eyes. My anxieties redoubled. However—the irritation of that hot inward blush, the stinging
rash in the mind, seemed in some manner to recede with
the long sense of leisure extolled by the river's evening
presence. A feeling of welcome melancholy followed the
hotter pain. Sadness heavy and yet as empty as the extending emptiness of evening, the widening of the sky,
the cooling of the earth, the lifting of the day's substance
that seemed to leave such an echoing wide emptiness in
the hours before the darkness. I felt all the yearning that
plays like music at the end of day. How beautiful life
could be—if I was not me! How beautiful life had been,
in the past, in a past so far yet so nearly visible as up
there high in the east the last true blueness of the day still
lingered. Leaning back without occupation in the back

seat by a now silent Mrs. Lawlor, leaning back opposite
the others rowing now easily and gently, my mind quietly
and almost with pleasure tasted the loss of hope, acclima-
tized itself to surrender.

Nobody spoke. Bradford and dark Richard pulled silently with a restful, homeward ease. Mrs. Lawlor sat with
her face turned away, also lost perhaps in thoughts of
other days, while her thin freckled hand dangled in the
cool water gliding away beneath the boat's stern. We
passed, now and then, groups of houses and bungalows
owned by riverside dwellers. Wooden houses painted white
and hung with creeper whose narrow lawns stretched
restfully to the wood-boarded water; on the lawns lay
cushions, or cretonned wicker chairs stood about; inside,
through the veranda posts, one could see an oil lamp light-
ing monotonously the planked walls within. Indeed, over
all these houses—though they might lie in flower-filled
gardens or show suddenly a light, or give the sound of
laughter, or reveal a group of people taking drinks on
the lawn—over all there lay nevertheless a shadow of
monotony; something bred of the low-lying ground, of
the age of the river, of the sadness of moisture and of
that pervading peace which sometimes falls too strongly
to be called content. Often the sounds of wireless and
gramophone came across the water; this distant river
music holds such a sad, lost note—is it perhaps the legacy
in our minds of summer nights of early bed in childhood,
when one was imprisoned but could not sleep for the light
evening, and when one heard sounds of music or of others
enjoying themselves brought more than ever clearly on
the warm, windless air? Only high in the sky lay salvation,
for there the day still lingered, and in its blue presence
not only marked an end but promised a renewal of itself.

At long last the little town came into view, and soon we were bumping gently against the landing stage, greeting the old boatman's hook with sighs of pleasure, balancing out of the boats onto firm land where the feet felt strange even after that most gentle, imperceptible roll of a flat-water boat.

Cream-painted and welcoming with gilt lettering, with flowered window box, with glossy black sign, stood the Crown. Lights already in the bar.

How simply the mind's upsets can be relieved by some small physical assuaging, by temporary catharses, by cool hands of the lightening moment! The world throbs with hot temper, heads that ache, hearts wrung with injustice —yet all these and the deeper ills that breed may recede before minor analgesics of the body, not of the mind. A hospital of weather changes, sudden sunshines and cooling rains, mountain airs and forest stillnesses, breezes of the sea and calms of the landlocked pastures; caffeines and tannins, witch hazels and soothing herbs, drafts of wine and shots of spirit, fumes of nicotine, musics, perfumes, caresses—a hundred matters to smooth the ruffled senses. And one of these is even cold water. It was thus with me that evening. I had a thorough wash. I lost myself in the water-clean basin, smelled refreshing soap smells and the soap's lathering blanket, buried my face in the pure fresh white towel, escaped from the world in that towel, emerged and ran the comb neatly through my hair, breathed with relief and sanctity in that white womb of a wash place with its locked door and perfect quiet. I felt no end better.

And I felt better still when in the adjoining bar I sensed my stomach expand with the pleasurable weight of a pint of iced lager—golden bubbles tickling over the

dry tongue, smooth musk-dry flavor. With no effort whatsoever, I was able to look up at Charley Diver standing
beside me and suggest, with a real smile, that we drink
another one. Charley bent his chin into his chest with
pleasure—then stammered, with eyes popping suddenly
round, possibly to denote question:

—Excellent idea, excellent. But this is my round! Have
this on me!

—On *no* account. Won't hear of it, Charley. Drinks are
on *me* tonight, this is my party, remember.

His eyes stayed popped at this for a fragile fixed
second before he looked down; his hand had meanwhile
gone to his pocket; but the idea that I was to pay for all
the drinks all the evening decided him. I think he knew
that he had better not intrude upon this—for fear one
breach would lead to another. I took the opportunity to
order the drinks—though through my mind there ran for
a moment the consideration that perhaps I had involved
myself too rashly; but then suddenly an idea of swelling,
exciting importance occurred to me. I remember looking
stock-still at a stone bottle on the shelf opposite, as if its
startling stoneness among the glass had itself prompted
such an unusual idea. And then my brain began to work
like a hot little pump compounding on this idea and all
its implications.

I had simply, suddenly, decided to make Diver my
friend, my intimate friend! And I turned with what felt
like a fluttering motion towards the large man standing
emphatic and colorless against the light of the lattice
windows.

I had not of course forgotten the main predicament.
But it was thrust with curious ease to another plane of
my mind, disregarded though stored. I was able at one

time to think of Diver in as many as three almost separate ways: first as the companion of this pleasant moment of drinking, as just a man standing beside me at a moment of ease; secondly, and more remotely, with reasoned dislike, as a rooted enemy—yet one that for the moment I had no wish to fight; and thirdly as a new figure in a savory plan, a plan that promised unimaginable excitements. Broadly, this plan invoked Diver as a friend; thus the lover of my wife was my friend; I can see now how plainly I welcomed sensations of injustice and torment more refined than any I had yet suffered. This was to drink the cup dry, to be deceived by one's best friend, it put one somehow more in the right. What insufferable duplicity, what a black, impossible burden for a man to bear! I was the victim to a degrading, abominable rending of all trusts . . . even then as I thought of it my lips would have tightened, a smarting dry anger have risen in my throat—only to be replaced instantly, as Diver began in a friendly way to tell me a certain anecdote, by a soft acquiescence as the part I had to play assumed control.

The ladies were away putting themselves in some order, the boys and Bradford in the wash place. We stood alone up at the bar, near a door hung with the blue and white programs of old regattas. The bar ran lengthways along towards a bow lattice window, with a window seat covered in faded pinkish flowered stuff. Against the light the grayly silhouetted head of the barmaid was bent over a newspaper; she kept herself quite still, except for her hand, which twisted the knob of a wireless set as she read —as if she had no hope of finding what she wanted. Another newspaper rustled in a dark corner by the window; but it was difficult to see who was there. The unseen creak

of a wicker chair. Otherwise in that long narrow room
with the air of a boat on dry land, yet always pervaded
by the damp green smell of the river, there was no movement. Sometimes the muted wireless played an orchestral
note, then spoke a sentence of commentary, then louder
announced some giant contest of amateurs, then lapsed
into a staccato burr of French. The little yellow light in
the wireless was the brightest thing in the room, glinting
to suggest that inside it lay some huge enchanted room
full of vigorous life. Nearly against the window a thousand white midges sprayed and whirled, making a moving
halo round the bent head of the barmaid. But such was
the hush—and these midget signs of life intensified the
stillness of us large humans—that at first we spoke almost
in whispers. But as again our glasses clinked, and as we
felt that no attention was paid, our voices rose. And at
the end of Charley's anecdote I found myself laughing
out loud.

Then all at once the ladies came in. They also were
laughing. They came in, three, secure in their number, as
though the bar was their possession utterly, laughing and
rustling and patting themselves in a way that suggested
disapproval of any others who might be already in the
room. And when they had greeted us, and were finally sure
of the relative emptiness of the bar, they all separately
gave sighs. 'So that's all right,' they seemed to say. Then
suddenly Mrs. Lawlor gave a low note of dismay. The
others turned startled:

—But where are the boys? And Mr. Bradford? Where
*are* they?

Charley said quickly:

—Just washing. They'll soon be along.

Mrs. Lawlor sighed and smiled downwards, putting her head on one side, a tragedy averted:

—Then that's all right then.

They talked, saying nothing. Madge said how very much better she felt, and now she was ready for *anything*; and wasn't it clever, just the thing for the river, to put the lights round the bar in little lanterns? Charley agreed, hugely. Mrs. Lawlor was pleased to be sitting down again, she wasn't sure the river air was good for her back—but anyway she'd had the nicest day for years. Charley winked that a little of what she fancied would do her good. Craig alone said little, but smiled strongly or nodded wisely when anything was said; once she got up and walked over to the window, took a broad scanning look in each direction, apparently saw nothing, and returned steadily to the company. Meanwhile I was ordering drinks, handing them round with a certain pompous joviality. I was playing the host, and in the ascendant. More than anyone else I was at the center of the gathering, the others toasted me with their glasses, I twinkled mine back to them. I was eager to ask again and again if that was exactly what they wanted: was it too strong, too weak, would they like water? Once Diver slapped me on the back. Madge said I seemed to be having a very good time—at which everyone laughed in a burst. I was the center of attention, and made sure that I remained so.

The boys and Bradford came in—and all over again the greetings were made, and the drinks ordered. We talked, and always with agreement. When any impersonal subject was raised, such as: 'These river pubs always make a packet of money' or 'Of course, punting's an art,' there was instant agreement, nobody thought of expanding or reducing the subject. But when, for instance, Madge ventured they must have rowed for at least three miles there and again back, there was immediate dissent, each had ready a different mileage and all manner of ingenious measurement.

Suddenly there was a shuffling and voices outside in the corridor. A woman's voice highest, commanding, thanking. The doorway became a person. Norma.

She stood in the dark doorway for some seconds poised, as if about to dive. This was not the ordinary Norma, something about her radiated, there was a suppressed glitter of a new kind, her glasses flashed, her mouth stayed stretched in a delighted smile, close gold earrings glinted the same amusement, her bosom rose and fell quickly under a starched white blouse. She stayed thus for some seconds, waiting until every eye was upon her—already some were crying 'Norma!'—then with an abrupt surge forward came very quickly into the bar. Her shoulders moved as she walked, primping and pumping with inward pleasure:

—Hello, everybody!

Everybody said 'Hello, Norma.' Some were already beginning to question her on the time it had taken on the train, and which train, and how far the station was—but she paid no attention. More discriminating, dark Richard said:

—Now what's biting her?

—Like to know, wouldn't you?

That came back swiftly at him, with a blink of her glasses—one knew she had closed her eyelids in mock secrecy. Bradford said, in a sinister tone:

—New hat, new costume, new blouse. . . .

—Bought it yesterday. Had to celebrate! Hi, miss, double gins all round—on me! Or would someone like Scotch?

There was a dead silence. This last trump had congealed them all. I alone moved. I muttered:

—I say, you mustn't really—this is *mine*.

—No, Mr. Bishop—this is *my* day.

—But it's *my* day.

—That's where you're wrong—it's *mine*.

Then I nearly said again that it was mine, but it sounded too childish. I fell back silent. Meanwhile Norma had started to hand round the drinks and everybody had started laughing and guessing what had come over her. I was winded.

—Come into a fortune, giggled Mrs. Lawlor.

—Come home and say you *found* half a crown? said Bradford.

The barmaid had put down her paper. Norma gave her a drink too—she accepted a port and herself began to smile, infected by the commotion and Norma's tremendous self-assurance. She put her hand to a switch and all round the bar those colored fairy lights came to life. And Norma ordered another round of drinks. She drew from her bag a thick roll of white paper notes, paper like writing paper, Bank of England notes.

—You don't mind a fiver, do you?

This was too much. A gasp of silence went up. Then Diver said:

—Now come on, Norm, this is enough. You can't do this to us, we're not as young as we were. What *is* it?

Norma looked round once more smiling secretly, and to make sure that everyone was listening, took a deep breath and began. Once begun she never stopped:

—It's all because of Nettie that's Nettie Lumley that used to do the bath requisites and tissues next to my beauty counter well poor Nettie did I tell you had trouble

with her insides she was never too well it was something
a wee bit dropped I think but really it wasn't that that's
not what I'm coming to though of course it was in a way
because it was because of this that she had her awful accident the one I'm going to tell you about of course it
happened weeks ago perhaps I did tell you or didn't I?—
She took another breath, not hiding it, compressing
her lips:

—Well if I didn't what happened was one day in the
kitchen at home they live in a self-contained down Croydon
way just she and her poor mother now she I pity well
there was Nettie cooking something for herself all alone
one dinnertime when Mum was out visiting her sister or
was it just down to the shops I forget but Nettie was all
alone and cooking up some herrings I think it was well
she's a clumsy girl begging her pardon but she is no
offense meant to her poor thing and the doctor who came
afterwards said the floor had a lot of fat slopped on it
you know how fat cakes up on a floor and goes like candle
grease when it gets cold you should always wipe it up
immediate so there it is this fat on the floor and what
happens but suddenly Nettie comes over queer and she
has a pain and this pain is sharp she says like a knife
cutting into her and so sudden and everything goes black
she doesn't remember a single thing—

Norma stopped to take a quick drink at her gin, there
was scarcely a second between her stopping, kissing the
glass to her lips, and starting again:

—It must have been a whole hour before they found her
and there she was lying on the floor with blood on the
side of her head and her body all twisted she must have
fallen down there and then and hit the gas stove she must
have come a crack they said afterwards there was hairs

and bits of skin on the gas taps and on the regulo too but we won't go into that it turns you up anyway but it was the old plate rack that broke her leg has anybody got a cigarette—

I fumbled in my pocket, but Diver was quicker. Then, while Norma was fingering this packet of fresh white fingers, Craig for once spoke. She said what one or two of us wanted to say. In her staid voice that deprecated fuss:

—But, Norma, what is this all *about?*

In a flash, as though she had never stopped talking, which in her mind she must not have done, Norma primped, though quite pleasantly:

—Patience and perseverance made a bishop of his reverence. . . .

—But, Norma!

—Curiosity killed the cat—

And then without waiting even for a light she was off again:

—So there's poor Net with a broken leg and fainted away oh I didn't tell you she caught her leg on the old plate rack the wooden one that was laying against the wall because only a day or two ago her mum had bought one a new one chrome finish much healthier they only need a wipe down and Net cracked her leg against the old one that wouldn't have been there but for this new one at all and of course if she'd just fainted she would have gone down careful the way you do when you faint away it was the fat that did it a contribution like—

—Norma, for heaven's sake . . .

—All right, L. H., all right we know you're there. *Eh bien* as they say in Frenchy France to cut a long story short Nettie's mum comes in and finds her and of course she nearly passes out too but doesn't not quite she keeps hold of herself and gets a doctor and there's Net safe in bed and awake but with a broken leg what do they do but say it's like a multiple fracture and she has to have it all covered over with plaster and lay in for weeks with it I shouldn't be surprised if it hadn't turned funny with hitting that old plate rack septic the thing was if you ask me—

—Norma, for heaven's good sake I am asking you . . .

It was Bradford again, and what he wanted really was to light Norma's cigarette, he had already burned his fingers with one match, the second was out, and now he held a third straight in front of her eyes. She pouted the cigarette into the flame and sucked forcefully, without raising her hand to steady it. And then without looking at Bradford went on with the cigarette bobbing up and down in her lips:

—That was back in April I said it was months ago didn't I and so Net had to lay up all that time well her mum was a real sport about it though I wouldn't be sure it wasn't to save herself a bit of trouble on the quiet too anyway she writes to her brother's sister-in-law that has her home in Skegness and sends Net leg and all up there for the air so there's Net cut off from all of us for weeks and with her leg all done up and I should think it itches fit to kill you but there really she's getting about a bit too you can in that plaster but Mum doesn't know this oh no Mum thinks she must be kept quiet as a mouse and the silly old witch ahem doesn't even send up her letters thinking they might upset her Net—

Richard lost patience and with his full dark serious force said, above the mock yawns and exhaustion that the others were simulating quite openly:

–Norma, will—you—please—come—to—the—point—
Norma stopped fascinated. And then brightly smiled:
–I know what *you* want. Miss, same again all round.

But while the barmaid, who had half returned to her
paper, started twisting the little tap below the gin bottle,
Richard repeated, now set in his purpose:

–Thanks very much BUT . . .

Norma looked round at them all delightedly:

–Oh, didn't I mention Net and I used to do our pools
together? I shared with Net every week. Well you won't
believe it but all these months there's been a letter on
Net's mum's mantelpiece to say we won not a penny less
would you believe it than four hundred and forty-three
pounds. Net came in with the cash yesterday!

The atmosphere became in an instant animated. The
idea of such good fortune—which must have suddenly
seemed possible for everyone present—enlivened the fairy
lights, a sudden gold tooth in the mouth of the barmaid,
the bubbles in the glasses, the faces and smiles and ap-
plauding eyes seen through the friendly blue smoke of
cigarettes. Norma was congratulated all round, and
round again. And she bought more rounds of drinks. She
described how she had felt, how Nettie Lumley had felt;
and others described how they would have felt. She was
fairly and squarely the center of all attention.

I too felt at first pleased for her—especially as after
that past conspiratorial meeting I felt vaguely that this
good fortune had something to do with myself—but I had
to take a back place, I knew the evening as I had planned
it was spoiled. No longer the host. Once I suggested dinner—when I might have hoped in some degree to retrieve
my ascendancy. But no one would dine. There were sandwiches and odd pieces of fish and crab on lettuced toast

at one end of the bar, and at these things people nibbled.
I drank little. But the others saw that Norma's pools
could be made an occasion, and they began to drink more
than usual. Madge not so much; yet her natural vivacity
rose easily with the general spirit. Mrs. Lawlor changed
soon to port, the two boys began to drink large mugfuls
of beer. Time passed, and as more local people arrived
we took our drinks out into the garden; there among the
trellises and by wooden steps down to the river we sat in
deck chairs and as a party achieved our own luminescence
against the dusk slowly and sadly falling on the river.

However, it was still light when, perhaps an hour later,
perhaps more, I suddenly found myself sitting alone with
Bradford and Mrs. Lawlor. The rest of the party seemed
to have wandered off into the twilight or back into the
bar. Across the river on a gap of flat meadow a low white
mist had started, and several cows had been walking
through this so that it seemed they had no legs: these
Mrs. Lawlor had seen, and nodding forward, thinking
they were horses, had started some reminiscence of a
cavalry regiment her brother had joined when she was a
girl and still in her pinafore. It had taken Bradford some
time to convince her that those legless creatures opposite
were cows, I had become absorbed in it too—and now suddenly looking up I found the party dispersed. Instantly
it occurred: Who was with whom? And I saw the sur-
rounding twilit garden with a quickening of anxiety. It
was very quiet. A laugh came across the water: then silence. I looked away and up the lawn to the hotel, its
lights shone winking yellow from small windows half covered with creeper, disguising heaven-knew-what warmths

and strange faces, gleam of glasses and knowing laughter. I rose and excused myself.

It was ridiculous—there was no one in the bar, what had suggested so much life contained now no more than the barmaid and one elderly gentleman smoking alone. There was smoke on the air—it had the feeling of a place vacated abruptly a moment before; it seemed that everybody had suddenly flown from me—having waited until my very appearance on the threshold. I went out again to the garden, and began to wander round the side of the house and along small shrubbed side paths that led nowhere. After the yellow-lit bar it seemed lighter outside than before—the darkness was holding off interminably and there had even crept into the sky a false new warmth, a sudden rosiness of sunset. I came to a little gate that opened on a cindered path leading along the river—it seemed a likely way for people strolling, I passed through and started along. I glanced anxiously to left and right as I walked, but remembered to keep my head forward; no one should think I was searching.

The path led through half-cultivated land, a wasted prodigal place. It was roughly cindered, flanked with a straggling of alders and tall weeds; occasionally piles of disused boat machinery and petrol cans appeared in sudden rusted pyramids; once the path widened for a derelict car park grassing up to a closed rusticated tea shack; then a new salmon-blood bungalow with a low roof and a garden of clay half-made; then an old boat builder's shed built of dark creosoted wood. And always through the leaves to one side one caught glances of the river and felt its sudden drop and near smell.

Suddenly from this undergrowth leading to the river there emerged two figures. As they saw me they made a

move back—but knew they had been seen, stood ir-
resolutely for a second, and then came walking towards
me. Craig and Dicky Carter. Craig was hitching self-
consciously at her blouse. Dicky's face looked hotter and
pinker than usual. But it was he who spoke:

—Hello, we were just thinking of a bathe. Then we
thought not.

I knew they had thought not, not at all. But I said
no doubt it was very muddy in there by the alder roots,
and then told them the best place was back in a chair on
the lawn. I myself was just taking a stroll—had they seen
any of the others? They had not. I began to move forward
and said I would see them later and those two were plainly
glad of this chance to go on too—they jolted away. And
I wandered on, more troubled. To think, of all people, this
Craig girl, whose plainly good-looking face seemed so
scrubbed clean of desire? And pink Dicky with pieces of
thistle leaf sticking to him? Was it that the normal was
most suspect? Or—was the evening such that it seduced
even the normal? How could one guess, how could one
*know?* How indeed could one *know* among so much confusion . . . ?

The path suddenly ended and I was out in the open
with a broad perspective of river in front. But as instantly as I was out, I retreated. But only a step—back
into the safe shadow of the alders. Madge and Diver were
standing close together, silhouetted against the steel lilac
of that evening sky.

Water stretched broad all round, it was a weir. A
broad triangle of sullen, flat, heavy water. They stood
by a hulk of lockwood that rose blunt-ended like the tiller
of a wooden man-o'-war. Two quiet still figures, Diver
and my wife, not moving, looking at each other. As I

watched, Diver moved slightly forward and reached for her hand; this was given him gently, easily.

I pressed back in the alders, breathed more quickly, throbbed indeed with silent breath. The two stood up there by the lock gates in a romantic attitude like two lovers embarking on an endless journey at the finale of a film, hands grasped, a bright twilit sky beyond. All round them the flat waters—in their very stillness roaring more than the streams of water that poured through the weir. That pouring water oozed from the weir channels beneath them like bands of molten green glass; though it poured at tremendous speed, it seemed set—like frozen oil. Moss on the immense wooden piles, heavy rust on the iron bolts and winches made a barrier of strength: but at any moment then I felt that the great dammed river would break through.

I thought: There, with my friend, my friend Diver! And just then Diver leaned forward and kissed Madge.

For a moment the kiss held, I broke cover and started forward. They were a hundred yards off. I had taken three steps when their two heads parted. Madge's laugh came echoing over the flat water. They turned and started to walk towards the path.

I bolted back into the shadow, suddenly terrified to be found watching. I turned and ran back down the cindered path. Blundering along, hot-faced and ashamed, indignant and powerless, I ran as fast as I could, only stopping when I reached the gate—to stroll onto the hotel lawn with a boiling unconcern. Five minutes later, from a window in the bar, I watched Madge and Diver come out from the path and stroll peacefully across. I remember nodding to myself, tightening my lips. *At last I knew.* I could formulate a direct action. But first—time to think.

The others were all again congregated in the hotel, tired now and sprawled in armchairs round the hotel's dark lounge. I suggested we should make for the cars—my wife and Charley, I said, were just coming in.

Then we drove back to London in silence, tired with the open air, sleepy with the falling night.

# 7

It meant pleading a headache and tiredness when we got home, then a night almost without sleep, then an early furtive rising to write with shaking hot fingers an urgent letter to myself from the directors of Violetta requesting me to attend a hairdressing convention at Birkenhead.

This letter I left obviously on the dressing table, and then I wrote a note for Madge. I left at eight o'clock, ostensibly to catch an early train north, and took the bus down to leave my bag in the little room I had used before. I went on further south to a main line terminus hotel where I could breakfast. 'Must get to the station by 8.30' I had written in that note. And it was in a way satisfactory—even then when my mind was hot with enacting and re-enacting that awful kiss—to have followed this false intention at least to the letter. Yet now this was not as before a serious need; my conscience had receded, I was now I knew without doubt in the right, I was for action.

But what action I was not sure. I sat in the great soft-carpeted space of the terminal restaurant and sipped my coffee. I can see myself—a small figure by the side of that immense marble-veneered pillar, bowed like the other solitary business men huddled here and there over the white tablecloths, over their silent papers. I had no paper —only a vast newsprint of thought. To speak to Madge? To speak to Diver? To disappear, taking with me every mobile resource? I kept on coming back to the necessity of doing something *at* Diver. At least of facing him, insolently, savagely—which in any case would lead to the violence I needed.

This indeed I had thought earlier, at eight o'clock, as I had crept into the dry long library and made instinctively for a small red book untouched for years. It was— I can see now—a ridiculous book: but it was one that at times I had built great dreams from, it was for me a curiously comforting book. It was a strong-man book, a manual of muscular development. Once I had seen a promise of great strength in a few weeks, a short cut. Even in that moment of anger I remembered the fact of Diver's size compared with my own bony weight. As I turned the pages my mind played with recollections of pictures of French boxers kicking—that might be a way: and of the queer magic of jujitsu—could one learn that? Never for a moment then did the idea of a weapon—even a broken bottle, a chair, a poker—suggest itself to me.

But the book had its effect. Already I felt more capable. Photographs, testimonials, and graphs made the process seem so simple. So simple one could discard it. I felt stronger. I began to eat with relish the cold sausage, the tomatoes. My jaw felt firmer, I looked up suddenly at the room, at the waiters whose eyes a moment before I could not have met. Now they could be met with hate, strong hate. I raised my hand and flicked a finger. The bill came. I left a deprecating large tip before walking steadily from the room. At the door I remember pausing; I stopped dead, standing on my two feet, and in the middle of the threshold took out a cigarette and at leisure lit it. I would move for no one. And as the flame flickered through— I saw with displeasure that my hand was nevertheless still shaking—the thought recurred with a calm surety: 'It can be done. *It—can—be—done.*'

It was already ten o'clock. I stood on the immense parapet outside the station and looked for a moment at this day and the street below. The traffic was already bustling with urgent, directionless clamor—this was a junction of several main roads. Rattling belling trams mixed with buses, shivering heavy beer lorries rumbled above the ferret bonnets of saloon cars crammed with small merchandise, railway horse drays tugged along by cyclists and red post vans and motorcycles. This intersurging mob of rattle and clang suggested a thousand different directions—I could not quite think what road I should take—and already the heat was tensing. High above the dust and vapor, above the old grimed brickwork and the hoardings, the sky expanded a breathless blue ceiling; not a cloud; it was going to be hot; a lightish haze trembled on all the circular horizon. Then suddenly I remembered what had for some minutes been at the back of my mind—the idea of a certain shop some streets away. I had noticed it on the afternoon I had danced with Norma.

To a person who is normally in much company, hours of enforced solitude connote hours of indecision, of an unbearable restless condition of not knowing what next to do, of the shiftless inability to choose any of a hundred dull alternatives. But it can be the opposite. When a man is alone and used to being alone, social burdens recede— he can make the choice he wishes with exact consideration. He can concentrate, evolve eccentric but determined courses which he is at liberty to follow with all his energy. No criticism, no contrary convention, no obligation forbids. In such airy cocoons the eccentric breeds and pursues his pure way. Thus a month before I would have entertained no heresy of strange behavior: but alone with my thoughts for weeks—and thus in the greatest sense alone —I was able to do exactly what I wished with concentration. So I concentrated on finding that shop. Soon I was standing opposite the window and re-reading the notice. It meant, but did not make, sense.

'PALIAKOFF'S SCHOOL OF GYMNASTICS—BE TWICE the Man you are in HALF the time.'

Red daggers of electric strength were drawn round the prospectus beneath; at each side of the varying black type stood the figure of a short-necked male god of prodigious torso and bicep, dressed only in skintight bathing trunks of much potency. There was an address beneath, it was not far away—I decided to walk. What follows now seems ludicrous, out of all sensible proportion. Looking back, it was ridiculous to consider such a project: but *then* it was different, my nerves were wrong all reasonable values distorted.

Paliakoff's was found in a back street of Italian cafés, radio accessory shops and small private companies. These were old houses, of the eighteenth century, crumbling and converted. Film companies showed lurid posters, the radio shops were painted with scarlet—but Paliakoff's had only a dark brown door. In the empty, dusty window stood several grimed display cards, a pair of boxing gloves and a truss grayed with exposure to some airless weather inside. It seemed empty, shut, and I felt a certain sense of relief. Yet it was irritating—for once I decided to do something, and here it eluded me. I rattled the door-

knob with a sort of petulance—and it opened abruptly
to show a tiled passage full of movement and noise.
Thwacks, bumps, groans, hoarse breathing came from
somewhere beyond; the entrance passage was filled with
men sitting on long benches waiting. Other men in gym-
nastic vests erupted suddenly from swing doors, disappeared springily through others. Paper notices of contests
and fights hung on boards on the walls; these all rustled
as I stood in the open doorway. All the eyes of the waiting men, men with square-held shoulders and cocked hats,
turned on me—in the doorway light they looked like a
pale-eyed row of prisoners. I was appalled. But then I
gathered all my determination and walked along the passage to a small grill marked INQUIRIES.

A bony man with cropped hair sat there in a vest. He
raised his eyebrows, opened his mouth in a stretched set
interrogative expression. I began to explain that I had
seen an advertisement, would like to know something of
the course and the terms—but in the middle the cropped
man turned his head away and shouted through some
doorway:

—Tony. Customer!

And before he had finished the swing doors had opened
and there bounced through a small but very broad man
dressed in a vest and white trousers. He bounced to a
stop a few inches from me, expanded his chest, smiled a
giant's splitting smile made of both false and gold teeth,
and introduced himself as Sergeant Paliakoff. I made my
inquiry again—but now trying to keep this impersonal, as
though I were inquiring for someone else. In Paliakoff's
small eyes upward turned there shone a bright fire of
energy, the zest of a fanatic. He began to bounce off,
beckoning to me.

–Come and see for yourself. See for yourself, sir. Five
shillings a class, class of one hour. Get you fit in no time,
half the time. Eight and six private class. There!

He had pushed the brass rail of those frosted-glass
swing doors and great space and sound opened up. The
gymnasium. A lofty room floored by wooden boards and
lit by a skylight. The walls were fretted with wooden
exercise bars, from the ceiling hung long dangerous-
looking ropes, the floor thumped with the movement of
some thirty or so vested men. Half were gathered together
in a drill squad, bending knees and breathing with arms
suddenly outstretched. Others pounded each other in corners with boxing gloves. One man slithered up a rope with
horrible agility. Others hung upside down on the parallel
bars or took flying dives off a springboard onto a leathern
horse. All manner of trestled racks and torturous machines seemed to fill this hollow place resounding with
crashes and thumps. The expressions of the exercisers
sweated with pain. Teeth everywhere gripped clenched,
bodies twisted and strained themselves while they grunted
and groaned. Memories filled me of stripped embarrassment on bathing beaches, in swimming baths.

As from the corner of my eye I saw a man crash astride
the horse with, it seemed, a crotch of iron, I took out a
notebook.

–Most interesting, it does indeed interest me greatly.
Now if you'd be so kind as to repeat this address, I'll make
a note of it and write to my friend.

Sergeant Paliakoff gave me the address, repeated his
terms, repeated in fact everything he had already said,
and I began edging back to the door. Suddenly I shook
hands with him and left. I walked as fast as I could round

the corner, saw a large tea shop, edged in and with a sigh ordered a cup of tea.

Then of course I began to revile myself for shirking that one definite move. But soon I was explaining that the gymnasium had reminded me of unpleasant times at school, that such an atmosphere would in any case have been unbearable—its mental oppression reducing any physical benefit. I began to appreciate my intuitive wisdom. A conquering retreat.

With the tea untasted I walked out again into the street. But there those momentary gratifications evaporated, the street suggested the day, the day suggested the long hours in which what I had to do must be decided. The heat of the now noonday sun had become oppressive; and with it the stifling street essences—petrol, dust, warm paper, hot cloth. Brass, false silver, glass caught the sun and glinted with headache flashes among the grimed brick and plaster. The doorway of a public house stood open, cool inside and dark. I went in. Unusually, I ordered whisky, a large one. It tasted good.

For the next two hours, until three o'clock, without bothering to lunch, I drank. I drank slowly, but with precision—I knew my head well enough to take no strong dose of intoxication. But in a light, imprecise way I did become intoxicated—airily, as with laughing gas. At the same time my mind seemed to clear itself. Purposes remained, but things looked different; urgencies declined. I talked with several people, joked with them, and once recounted a successful anecdote. These people—I met several groups in different saloon bars—seemed to have no regular office hours to recall them, they seemed remarkably free and handled much money; not once did they try to cadge off me. I envied them their freedom and their happy-go-lucky untroubled air: and in envying, I might myself have assumed a part of it. I supposed them to be commission men of some sort, perhaps racing men, or even theatrical. Once two men and a woman asked me to come on to their club—a place they called the Blue Moon —for a drink after three o'clock. But I refused this— I am not quite sure why, except at the back of my mind must have lain a sensation of time running short—and thus I found myself once more out alone in the close glare.

I walked for some time along a main street, noticing in my clear inebriation things I never seemed to have seen before. So many people, so much summer body! There seemed to be many more glistening fat people than usual, collars opened to the heat, frowsy in summer dresses no longer fresh. Women wore more powder than usual, many faces stared caked with white like chalk; strands of sweat-damped hair straggled behind ears. I remember an old woman passed in a cream linen dress, wearing wool stockings and plimsolls—she stands out in the glare like a painted portrait. A man in braces sold plums, some of which lay squashed on stained paper. Pieces of paper and cartons and the rind of fruits caught the sunlight on the dust-gray pavements. Pink rock melted among stiff cardboardish ice-cream cones: there were no more ices. Ceaselessly the traffic drove by, cracking and spitting and roaring, and always quivering out more of its burning essences, etherous and blue. Cool people passed in shaded taxis, immaculate and separate. But on the street the color of every dress seemed dazzling bright, reflective of the sun's fierce light, and because in such heat one was more than ever conscious of the amount of cloth stifling the air. Empty fish shops looked cool, but stank. Above, on the canyon ridgeline of the street's buildings, the sun

immobilized each high window, each stone facing, so that
these appeared stiller and more impassive than in any
other weather. The blue sky above never moved, it blazed
in a rigid Italian grip. Such a day might continue forever. My shirt began to stick to my back.

The drink was souring inside me. My head began,
slightly at first, muzzily to ache. I saw a public lavatory,
tiled and sunless—I went in and down. Underneath, among
the tiles, in the aqueous gloom of the pavement lights, it
was cooler. Other men were there, but they stood inde-
pendently—the sense of crowd was gone. There was a
bubbling of irrigation water—and suddenly, very suddenly, almost as a revelation to my aching head, I realized
the presence of the pipes. Pipes I saw. They ran everywhere—white-painted pipes, gleaming copper pipes, old
dust-laden pipes, and all of them curling and branching
and forking like things alive and waiting; some suddenly
bulged, like snakes digesting a swallowed prey. The full
horror of plumbing came to me. Disintoxication in a
strange way sharpened my eyes—though much was muddled, certain objects obtruded themselves with startling
clarity. And I was instantly reminded of that other moment, in Diver's flat, when I had stood in the lavatory
during that first terrible party, baffled and foolish.

As if this recollection reached out for others my eyes
were drawn abruptly to notice that all round the tiled
chamber, at points of intersection above the pipes, there
occurred small glass aquaria bubbling with green water.
In each of these copper-bound glass tanks slept an old
copper beast, a round ball-like crustacean with one spider-
ous thin leg, a thing that never moved but pursued some
dark and secret hibernation, rusting and greening, growing barnacles of verdigris forever under water. I remem-

bered the aquarium tank in Diver's passage, how I had stood silently by it through the nefarious moments with Mrs. Lawlor and Bradford above. A rage of hate rose. I began to shiver. Almost running I remounted those stairs.

I think that was the first time that I began urgently to want to be at Diver, at Madge—urgently to attack. But as I came out from the lavatory cool into the sun, that hot air and the slow drag of time again struck— it was early still, those two would not be found, there was nothing to be done about it. The long afternoon dragged out ahead. And I began slowly, with painful stuffed head, to walk. A yellow thickness seemed to crust my mouth, I wondered for a moment where that place the Blue Moon might be. I did not know. A café? My stomach revolted at the tannic thought. I just walked.

The pavements passed. People hurried by: I had constantly to give way, shuffled and buffeted, useless among these others with a purpose. The traffic sickened the air with its vapor—always dust, sweat, petrol, a hot shimmering over everything. I remember keeping in near the glass-fronted shops. Dark and cool beneath the sunblinds: then the bright sun: then the sunblinds again. I kept skirting people looking into shops, I did not like to pass in front of them—yet felt affronted by having to shuffle round. Then there came a shop with no spectators. I stopped to look—for a breathing space. It was a hospital for dentures.

Mounted on shelves of black plywood the dentures sat and grinned. Each was isolated, crouched like a crab with indrawn legs. White pelleted teeth and harsh pink vulcanite. Secretive glints of steel and gold. Three small green cactus in pots lent their unearthly festivity, false as the teeth. White cards aggressive with black hand-penned script appealed and warned: INSTEAD OF USING POWDERED GLUE—WHY NOT HAVE YOUR DENTURES TIGHTENED? . . . WHY NOT BE PREPARED FOR AN EMERGENCY—HAVE A DUPLICATE SET IN PLASTIC VULCANITE AND STAINLESS STEEL?

And one card said ICI ON PARLE FRANCAIS—I could see all the teeth slowly move into motion and champ out litanies of the pen and the aunt, chew the declensions of avoir-to-have. And my teeth, I thought?

My teeth were yellow and long and now coated with stale morning. Was I old, was I dropping? I had no sharp white enameled clenchers like these here, teeth of the strong and young and white, potent teeth. Could I have these yellow ones out, surgically drawn, and smile with bright young bone again, flash potent messages to all? Would I love Madge? Would she me? More? What are those teeth of great Diver? Strong teeth? Flesh-biters? The fortunate, the giant, the fearless, the ginger. Was there no doubt but that his teeth looked white only by dint of the strong ginger mustache above them and the red beer-blue flesh that bristled purpling round them?

Passed along, out from dental shade to the sharp blind sunlight, in under shade again and round people and— suddenly the façade in film-emerald rough-cast of none other than the palace of tea dance where once I had danced with Norma! Where, to the pressure of her neat cold body, I tangoed a forbidden thought at a time when my business was to investigate the offenses of others. But with me that feeling had passed, had I not thrust it away? More sinned against than sinning? *They did it first.* With a clear conscience I had thrust it—though delightful—

aside. I was unquestioned. But we danced. And they thought me a thief.

Passed the starred posters of star bands, and now there were no sunblinds. With every hot step the aching muffled hotter my head, the sweat stuck about my shirt and my pants, there was no breathing clear. I paused again by a window—such cool things I had never seen. A florist's. Faded green paint, green garden paint inside, green wooden shelves and green wicker baskets of flowers, thin green tin vases. All leaves clustered wet round their flowers, the flowers glowed palely in the cool moist shade. A smell from the doorway of watering cans, of garden earth. Then there was nothing more I wanted than to go inside and stand there on the tiled floor, my head sensing these moistures craved—and feeling faint I went inside. The mixed perfume of the flowers hung strong on the shaded air; but lightly as at a flower show. A fresh-faced elderly woman with a watering can came forward in a green overall, brushing a wisp of gray hair from dry pink cheeks.

—May I help you?

I remember my surprise. They were the first words spoken to me for a long time. It freshened me to hear them, to be recognized again as a person and useful of this world. I remember smiling eagerly, and asking the prices of sprays and bunches. Together we moved round the shop. Water on the flowers seemed to breathe into my mouth, washing all yellow things away, leaving clear water, like water in a glass. Finally I bought a bunch of marigolds. Then I was out in the sun again. Aimless again I walked away, flowers in hand.

A banging, large, of cans. A huge vehicle mountainously drove up by my curb. Agile men jumped from it, dusty with battle. For a shocking moment the pavement was

charged with guerillas— I stopped dazed but saw then
that they were no guerillas but dustmen. Yet their attack!
Their strength! Their freedom! Heavyweights, they
laughed and shouted to each other, oblivious of the day-
time crowd, shouldering great cans to and from their
machine. I saw them plainly as the true rulers of the city,
the free aristocrats—vigorous, unafraid, freed of all vice
and vanity: once a dustman, all fetters fell, no more pre-
tense was needed, yours was the humility where true pride
may flourish. Fortunate men, ranging the streets with
their free limbs! Keen livers these—but I, Henry, was I
too not abased? Had I not been shorn of my vanities?
My face pressed in the dust? My love tossed to the can?
Had I anything left? Myself? Spirit?

Through the long hours I wandered on. Until it was
half past five. And then the doors of a clean-swept public
house opened and I went inside and blessedly slaked that
dry thirst. I sat, slowly drinking, seeing and feeling more
clearly, for what seemed a very long time.

It was seven o'clock when I rose. Still no course was
exactly clear—except a need now to be near home, not
away as I had planned in the morning, but near, watching. The Claverton Hotel occurred—there one could wait.
I walked to an underground station.

A quick look up and down the carriage—but there was
no one I knew—and so I settled down. No paper, I stared
in front of me. The light shone down bright, people opposite in a row seemed all to have their heads or their eyes
turned on me. I looked down at my boots—there crept
over me the sensation that I and always and only I was
being looked at, criticized, judged; I was the only person
in the world, all these others were phantoms in league

with the Creator, they were a society of knowing spirits from which only I had been excluded—and knowingly, amused as parents at a children's party, they winked between themselves and watched. I cursed myself for being such a fool, looked up to fix the stare of the man opposite, and quickly looked down again.

Between the last two stations I thought of that smoke tower in my own garden around which my own wistaria grew—was it on this line, was I passing underneath my own land now, under my own house, under whatever was happening in my own house? Tormenting scenes arose. They sprang up vivid in all their imagined detail—and then dully faded for want of *knowing*. But there returned the memory of that kiss, and of the skin of Diver's red thrown-back throat.

It was a walk of a few minutes from the station to the Claverton—two terraces and up a short hill. I kept my eyes down on the pavement all along that first terrace, persecuted still by the eyes in the train. When at last I looked up the street was blessedly empty, and there was the space of the first evening air. The beer had not fuddled but in its slow reintoxication had made one strangely alert. My eyes selected from the general view isolated objects which stood out and addressed me with unusual significance. Thus I saw instantly that along this particular terrace cats sat at the open summer windows, many cats. They sat quietly musing the evening air, each a separate heraldic figure—separate, but so many that they seemed to sit in silent colloquy. So many cats I had never seen before. And as I looked up at all those windows, there sprang out distinctly from the façades those pipes again, gutter pipes and drainpipes winding fantastically over the otherwise ordered house fronts of gray plaster:

many had been picked out in bright paint, others darker took on a depth of shadow cast by the lowering evening sun. Yet no people were about—and the quiet evening air, the open windows, the waiting cats and the still machinery of pipes suggested nothing but people, people who were away inside intent on preparing for the evening, cooking, dressing, washing. I alone was out and purposeless. And then I saw—it would have been the quiet air under a widening sky, the air of past summer holiday that made me see a certain porch out-jutting from one of the houses. An iron and glass canopy, erected specially for that house, portentous and announcing the doorbell. I was back under the porches of my own youth, porches where I had waited, excited and forlorn, attired for the visit. Winter porches lit for the party, pink dresses and dancing pumps bursting from overcoats, and the light shining in the hall through its warm frosted glass. And summer porches beyond which lay gardens to play in, cool rooms with jellies . . . and sometimes the doctor's black-shadowed surgery. Small and uncertain among those fearful excitements, I felt the sand in the bottom of the seaside bath, I heard music playing in the water pipes like music from a far-off band . . . joyful and uneasy . . . times to escape to but no more certain themselves than the present. . . .

But there, already, were the doors of the Claverton.

# 8

---

I went in, saw that none of those I knew were there, angled
off to the last corner of the bar, behind a great lampshade, where hidden I thus ordered my drink. A long
amber cool pint for the afternoon's mouth. Ensconced,
I gained courage, confronted the drinkers.

Drink soaks and time soaks, seed-gone idlers. In mack-
intoshless summer still brown, weak brown in the weak
electric shadow. Yet each one, one by one, whether dropping in on the homeward way, or coming out tired of
the room that was home, or just in for a chat, or exactly
in for a night of it, for a read of the paper to relieve the
outside or a slow-ticking feel of the rising beer to relieve
the inside—each one stood about a self, all engaged loiter-
ing with the clock moving behind. All predatory their
faces. Quick-eyed, down-mouthed, stiff-backed bristlers.
Women too. Teatime whores and their waiting wolves. All
attack, all nod. Cold-eyed laughter. Fierce laughter.

Easy, humored laughter—relaxing and loving each
other like brothers. Twinkling gentlemen ready to flirt

with the ladies, who are sporty. And why not? Faces hard-grained by day work, now they relax in leisure and the moment's pleasure, imbibing sweet cheer, healthful company of fellow creatures at the end of day. No argument but reflective views on life, over pipe, nod not of yes but of slow considering, no predatory ones these but the good English come to rest, growing pink in the warm glow of eventide. I love them.

I took a slow, long, reassuring pull at the amber in the ample glass. You could look at many people in many ways. Twenty minutes ago—what mood had I? In the tube? Almost in a fit. Then lonely and left out. Now lonely still but remarkably in. Now the exquisite sensation of armored loneliness, solitude desired and got, moments of picking the skin on feet, cleaning combs with some most sharp hairpin, cozy-contained without hurry, no fear, womb-happy. But lonely—lonely sad? Like those cats! The kitten that is left undrowned to comfort the mother is a lonely small blind kitten, brotherless and sisterless, more to be pitied thus lonely than the other wet ratlike five in the ashcan? Or not? To survive alone or die with fellows?

A long slow pull at what did really go down surprisingly nicely. Such a pink-shaded electric-bulbed gasolier of fortunetellers! Tall flamingos and green-billed high-steppers on the mirrors. Spoiling good mirrors with their paint, those high-steppers? In the mirrors two lights—winking night light, daylight through the door bolted open for the evening draft, daylight from the evening square in the doorway cool-blue and inviting, smelling of some perfumed tree, most cool against the hot beer-wood and brass within.

He in the bowler and dark suit would be a chap from
the city, youngish, drained white by his ledger, dropped
in for one with his open-necked friend. Open-necked? No
work? Night work? Engineer at waterworks? Nightwater-
work? Talking about the prices of things. And how settled those three at the table, two girls in summer dresses
and a man, a man in hot tweed showing braces beneath
that coat which must be his only one, summer and winter.
Girls talking hard to each other, heads together, breathless intimacy of I said to her I said. While the man talks
nothing, sits looking about, nothing to say. Slow drinkers,
they would be there for hours, settled in. Girl typists?
Sangster's waitresses?

But really they were no more than girls aged so-and-so
with private girl problems and girl dreams and no matter what their jobs arc. So the brother, so all the rest,
city bowler and waterworks white shirt, not what they
looked and did and dressed, but what was happening inside, individuals all, all at some stage of what all individuals did at some time or other like each other. Me for
instance, no beer drinker but drinking beer. Why? But
on such a hot night this was cool. Or whisky, a long, long
whisky? Or a short one, to pull up?

I looked down at my hand stretched mouse-haired white
on the polished scarred bar wood, that is, at part of me.
But it looked extraordinarily separate, like someone else's
hand, seen near with a glass. The effect of drink—I remember trying to warn myself to be careful. There was a
reason for being there, a need to watch and keep cunning—no one knew this better. And the predicament came
flooding back; to the gleam of old mirrors, to the never
moving lampshade, to the thick plush dust and the smoke
mist and the stale-sweet thickening air it declaimed itself

all over again. More detached and removed from myself indeed by the alcohol, I wondered exactly what I thought, whether I hated—at that moment—Madge? Or still loved her? Whether I hated Diver?

But this was difficult—for instance, it was difficult to think of Madge exactly without thinking of home. And thus of my own life. Was it then that I must have Madge to be myself? Could one exist only through the beloved, in her eyes and back again? Or was it only in the beloved that one had the chance of losing oneself, of escaping away? For instance—I contemplate Madge, I see there both someone I know and feel for and also someone who knows and feels for me and will receive me, unquestionably receive me, uncritically because we have become of one blood—and so uniquely I am permitted to lose myself, escape from all consciousnesses of self. No evidence that one did not want to lose rather than find oneself. No difference?

I took another drink. Why thus be jealous—because this loved one, this possession was being snatched away? Her snatched away or me snatched away through her? Or was it no snatching, was it the willing going of her that gave pain? The evidence of worthlessness in that which had been held so pure? The fall? The collapse of the angel? She whom I put all trust in went. She to whom I attributed all quality (Myself) was after all the same as all the others (Myself too?).

I took another drink, the glass showed only a soap of froth at its bottom. So another—a whisky. Then continued . . .

After that it is difficult to remember. One can recall only flashes, separate incidents in the confusion. I know

I drank slowly on, the clock away over the mahogany mirrors stretched its long arm over the white hour face. It grew to be eight o'clock, and eight-thirty, nine o'clock. And night fell, a fine violet summer night fell. The bar began to fill. Many stood by the door for the freshness. But the counter was full, others must have preferred still the security of the counter, the dusty glitter and the solid wood, the bottles and the movement, all the year round, summer and cold winter.

It must have been then, certainly not until then, that I began to lose serious control of myself. All day there had been a wavering, the day had insisted in different degrees to make some sort of a clown of me, aimless obstacles always had frustrated any moments of clear decision—but in all that I had managed a measure of control. But now I think this was going. Perhaps previously I had been erratic, now my mind was muddled beyond any but flashes of coherence. I do not think I was actively drunk—but rather dazed with drinking, with a slow sotting. I was ignorant of much that must have gone on outside the sphere of my lampshade. I did not, for instance, see when Dicky and Craig and Richard and Bradford came in.

They must have seen me long before I saw them. I expect I looked fairly far gone. Certainly none of them came up to greet me. Perhaps I was making too much of a fool of myself. I would surely have been muttering, smiling down at that hand, gripping the bar. I seem to remember gripping the bar to steady myself, though I was not lurching—I would have been perhaps a little off the balance of my feet, perhaps circling slightly with that circling motion not so much of unbalance as of soliloquy. This I can only suppose—but one has seen too many solitary drinkers, the solitary obsessed, to imagine one cannot look the same. Men perhaps soft in the head, perhaps too hard in the head on a single obsessive problem. So one has seen lifelong litigants, religious curb-strutters, the muttering solitaries of public libraries. But for all that I might really have been reeling. One thing I do remember—my gray Homburg was away pushed back on my head. I remember not caring about this.

So I do not know when or at what time I looked up and over the bar and there saw those four standing drinking beer by the door. But I do remember feeling immensely pleased; I think after the hours of solitude and with such an accumulated grief I simply welcomed the comfort of people I knew, faces to talk to, the reassurance of company. There was no question—I left my corner immediately, grabbed up the whisky and threaded my way, bumping, towards the door. Heaven knows whether they were pleased to see me or not—but we seem all to have greeted each other—and there would have been the usual talk of the heat and laughter at the cooling beer. I must have looked comical, I was talking a lot and there was the hat on the back of my head and the withering marigolds sticking from my pocket—I think Craig's face was looking at me intently, with the beginnings of a smile, and no doubt she had me already in the category of a man half-seas-over; a comic character in line with latchkeys and music-hall lampposts, who should prove amusing. The boys seemed more than usually cordial—I expect this was admiration; 'Old Bishop's got something in him after all.' Bradford was congenial as ever.

Nevertheless it was he who finally said words which I can hear now, ringing cold as a bell. It was all right until then. I think we were having quite a time, and I certainly

had momentarily forgotten why I was there at all. Then
Bradford said:

—Well, I must say you look in the pink all right, never
seen you looking so well!

Before he had finished I had stopped raising the glass
to my lips, I was looking shocked at his carious teeth
making a mouth of the words. The air seemed suddenly
to clear. I felt like an invalid robbed of his ill by an un-
comprehending visitor. The full disaster fell again on me,
but magnified, magnified. And overpoweringly then, an
immediate whim that flooded up huge, I found I had to
tell them. I had to have my illness recognized. I had to
strip myself. I had to have their sympathy. And with this
must have come that other urge—the desire of the deceived man to make public his cornutation, to perform
miserably and pitifully his great cornutation. Quite
clearly, with a sort of pulpit emphasis, still in some way
hesitating but knowing with no doubt that the words anyhow would spill themselves out, I said:

—Never looking so well? But how very little you know,
L. H.! Do you know who I am? Do you know *what* I am?

A pause. I can still hear the words resounding, far
away, as though spoken by somebody quite else. Surprising words:

—I am a man whose wife has betrayed him! A man
whose wife has a lover! A man whose wife is in the arms
of another man— Now!

A dead dreadful silence. They all stood and looked at
me. Then looked, embarrassed, away. I think Bradford
mumbled something about there being ladies present. But
there was nothing in me to care, I felt a stripped feeling
across my chest, I was being offered to them armorless,
and that other voice went on:

—For twenty years married, I gave her everything, every trust, every love, every faith. Now all this is thrown back in my face.

They must have tried to intervene, I expect they tried to laugh it off or change the subject, for then I said:

—I don't think you realize, I am talking seriously. They think they can fool me. *Me!*

And went on—I began to look at them one after the other, their faces I can see set and very clear, and perhaps then it began to come upon me that these were not friends but enemies, these of the set faces, critical, shocked, as though I had insulted them personally, faces of no shred of sympathy:

—Do any of you know what it means—to have built up a life through the years, the long lovable years, and then in a moment to have all that edifice made nothing? Simply by some swine that comes sneaking in for his own dirty pleasure, his bloody little lust . . .

The voice I heard in my ears was rising, I must have been shouting. But through this, even this, I heard Craig butt in suddenly:

—Have you heard about Charley, Charley Diver?

—WHAT?

Her face seemed to jump back alarmed. I had shouted at the top of my voice. I felt people all round me turning, there was a sudden quiet it seemed in the whole bar. Craig was saying haughtily, her little forehead crinkled with indignant offhandish lines:

—I only asked whether you'd heard about Charley Diver. . . .

—DIVER! Have *I* heard the news about MISTER DIVER!

Hot, blazing, the whisky and beer mixed in me—bright angry I saw how they were all against me. I must have

raved at them then. I told them how I knew the bloody
lot of them were laughing up their sleeves, I told them I
knew right enough. And I said something more—I said
how I was going to teach them a lesson, and Mr. Diver
a lesson, and that lesson was going to begin right at that
moment, a lesson none of them would forget. . . .

Then I was out of the door and striding hard up the
hill.

Fast up the hill, the avenue—as fast now as ever possible, no moment to lose. Dead in the center of the broad
pavement—a woman approaching seemed to scuttle aside,
looked over her shoulder nervously. But I hardly remember her. I must have been muttering. I do remember keeping my hands gripped close in my jacket pockets, making
an armory of the pockets, and the feeling of white-boned
knuckles and the wetness as those marigolds now crushed.
Now no porches of my youth, no troubling pipes, no godlike dustmen, all phantoms of failure had gone, swallowed
in what was a sightless wet tight rage.

Sightless rage—yet sighted sharp on a destination.
None of the plane trees mattered, no street lamps, no
pavement cracks that passed—my eyes were up towards
where the house was, I strained to see it long before this
was possible. All the long abusing of myself swung round
and up, revolted. Inadequate, ineffectual, unwanted, I can
see I had for so long past receded upon a lonely journey
whose road now turned out to be no lost thing of mac-
adam but instead a vicious rubber band that sprung me
now back with force. No wandering circular road—those
long distended nerves had snapped back to precision.
And I who seldom swear kept muttering over and over,

like an excretion on the tongue, that word '. . . bloody.
. . . '

Then at last the houses. Number 48 bare, a wide plaster
face eyed here and there with yellow windows—alive, like
a house with the painters in. And my own house farther
on, in darkness and obscured by trees. I passed Number
48, swung open my gate, and then stopped. No light on
at all. But speckling through the leaves a street lamp
showed in ghostly light the front door—and this was
open. It stood open and black, empty—with no light behind in the hall it meant unequivocally that the house had
been deserted. Yet Number 48 lighted—the connection
was obvious, the direction of the two drives asserted their
movement. Madge had slipped out of one door leaving
it open in hurry or in intimacy and had traversed those
drives, one out and one in, to enter that house of lighted
windows. I was away, she had discarded all care. From
where I stood it was difficult to see Diver's basement windows. But above for a moment the drawn blind of an
upstairs window shone out plain and there came back
silhouettes I had seen pictured in books or on postcards,
the black shapes of two figures approaching and seen
embracing: this for a moment—and with it out there by
the drive gates, in the lonely street lamp, that feeling of
exclusion briefly returned. But the next second I was
hurrying up the gravel of Number 48.

Past that flagstaff, straight down to Diver's side door,
stumbling against dwarfs and milk bottles, kicking them
ringing aside—and then stood before the shut door with
my hand raised to knock. But dark! Dark which was worse
than light—I saw hands extinguishing lights, hands on
switches to turn on the intimate dark: and I let my own
hand fall. I felt a secret possession of close cunning—

breathing heavily in the dark from that fast walk I turned and returned very quietly up into the drive. I went up the steps—Mrs. Lawlor's front door was left on the latch, but I peered carefully through its frosted panels. No one in the passage.

The lit emptiness only emphasized that people were much engaged behind doors. I pushed, the frosted panels without noise swung back. On tiptoe to the head of the basement stairs. Listening, above my own breathing. Dark down there in Diver's basement—but by a pale light from some half-open door I could make out the shape of the stairs, the blurred pattern of linoleum beneath. No sound. Very quietly I went down.

On the last stair it could be seen where the light was: not from Diver's sitting room, but from the bedroom end of the passage. I saw now it did not come from the bedroom—the half-open door of what looked like a larder showed its bare ceiling and one small, unshaded electric lamp. For a moment longer I waited. No sound. Then I stepped down onto the linoleum and crept towards the bedroom door. The damp basement smell seemed to enclose the passage as thickly as the silence, as heavily as my own held breath.

No light showed from beneath the bedroom door. I raised both hands, one to the doorknob and the other in a position to snap on the light as soon as the door should be open. Then I banged open the door and blazed on the light. The glare was dazzling. The room focused. It was empty.

Without waiting I swung out and clattered along the passage, burst open the door of the sitting room. Empty.

Then I turned and went back down that passage wrenching open every door on the way—opening all damp

cupboards and closets, old wine cellars and disused lard-
ers, all the subterranean holes that had formed part of
the old kitchens. Nobody in any of them, the doors stood
open all over the passage like wings confusing the air.
Once a broom fell out, once I faced that pipe-clustered
lavatory where weeks ago I had stood waiting—and in
this empty void, robbed of all object, I think I sobbed—
and a feeling of loss came welling back. I wrenched at the
last door, the door with the light. It was no larder but the
room in which stood, rusted but hot, the boiler that
heated water for the house. It was the last room. Something further than all else, some last cord of sense must
have snapped in my head—I can only remember reaching
forward at the boiler and grabbing at the long-handled
poking iron that was stuck in the boiler's front. It came
out thin and wieldy, a foot of it red-burning hot. Once it
clanged with an iron ring on the boiler pipe; I must have
tightened my grip, I remember being with it out in that
passage again.

Confused, not clear—a bad dream half-remembered.
There seemed to be a music beating inside my ears, right
on the drum a mad high-edged music whining: and clouding behind it a roar of avalanche, a maelstrom hum of
ceaseless waters poured, a thunder of deafness.

Suddenly, in all that turbulence, among so much moving sound, isolated on another sensitive plane, as when in
a nightmare some of the senses gallop yet others remain
curiously still, I caught sight of a real movement. Something else but me in the passage was moving. A light
movement, stealthy, as small as a glint of light, a wink,
but at that time expanded huge in my alerted eye. Then
I got it. It was the nervous glint of a moving fish.

I remember abruptly being above that tank with the

red glowing poker raised—and then this was plunged down with my arms in the water and among those fish. From somewhere—as the steam hissed and the glass shattered, I heard a dreadful high neighing noise, a mad noise—and this must have been from me. Glass crashed everywhere, and water and all that was in the tank broke out and down thudding and streaming and ringing on the floor. A fish fluttered wetly in the light—I raised my foot to stamp—then stopped, and that neighing like a guttural machine slowed and lowered itself gurgling and droning down into a long cough, a drawn staccato of deep coughing sobs. From deep inside my coat the sobs seemed to come, from the breast there, from the deepest tired layers they came coughing up like slow bubbles of air released from the blackest depth—the poker lay putting up a foetid burning from the linoleum, the water round it steamed, glass winked, fishes suddenly unsheathed themselves into the light and, wriggling, vanished.

Voices came down the upstairs stairs, women's voices and steps talking and coming forward to the square of light at the top of the stairs—as if inverted it was a downstairs landing of long ago and voices were coming up to the dark nursery—and then suddenly a click, light switched on all round. I looked up blinking to see standing there erect the purple dress of Mrs. Lawlor. But with Madge's face on top of it.

—Henry!

It cleared. Madge's face was over Mrs. Lawlor's shoulder, and now it came forward brushing aside the figure that had shielded it. Madge came down the stairs. Talking quickly, scattering words:

—Henry! What are you doing? Are you all right? What's wrong? You're wet!

From behind her halfway down the stairs, head forward, the voice of Mrs. Lawlor now not quavering but severe:

—There's a smell of burning.

I began to see where I was—leaning crouched against a table where the fish tank had been. I stared up at Madge and heard my voice repeating as if from a great distance of time:

—It's not me that's wrong, it's you.

—Henry, you're ill!

—It's you that's wrong, you and that swine—

—Henry!

—Carrying on behind my back—

—What *do* you mean?

Behind, the correct cold voice was repeating like some president judge:

—There *is* a smell of burning! Look at that water, look at the glass, everywhere it is . . . mess . . .

I somewhere raised a voice:

—Charley and you are doing things.

—There's fishes everywhere . . .

Madge had paused while, knelling, those words must have resounded into her comprehension: a look of shock took her face and dropped the strained concern from it, her eyes widened and her mouth grew loose.

—No!

That was my voice again, but now I think lowering, no more a force of meaning, it droned:

—No good, no good, I know, I've known for weeks. Down by the river, by the water you were kissing—I . . .

I saw Madge stiffen again. Her mouth hardened to speak distinctly, she looked like a nurse speaking without sentiment—but far back in her eyes there came some great compassionate softness:

—You stupid, you stupid—that was nothing, that was the evening, the party . . . Do you know what's really happened, where Charley really is? He's in hospital, he may be dying. And Norma's dead.

For a moment the words had no meaning. I remember repeating them, mouthing them like paper words:

—Dying? . . . Dead?

And Madge's voice relentlessly went on:

—Norma and Charley went away on that money. They had a bad accident in their car. Norma was killed. Charley was dragged out, he's in hospital very badly ill. Now— do—you—understand?

Then those words came crashing down with huge belling presence. I think I still looked up at her, single words came dropping from me, from nowhere:

'I' and 'didn't' and 'know.'

While from above Mrs. Lawlor's voice intoned with hard accusation:

—Yes, poor man, lying in hospital. And the police here about his trade plates. And you prowling about . . .

Suddenly from upstairs in the passage the front door battled open, footsteps and laughter sounded, then suddenly hushed themselves as if entering a hospital. Shuffling, a single voice, Bradford's, calling:

—What's up down there?

Instantly Madge was down the last stairs, arms wide embracing me, covering me as she called back over her shoulder:

—It's nothing, it's all right.

In a whisper, capable, fierce, to Mrs. Lawlor:

—Stop them coming. I'll see to this. We'll go—the back door. It's the heat, he's ill. Go back.

Mrs. Lawlor moved back instantly, commanded—and lowered what she was going to say to a whisper as well:

—Prowling about, we all knew it was him—

—Go back!

Without looking again Madge took me by the shoulders, half carrying me. We limped off down the passage and away. There was then about her an air of complete capability, a woman resolute in giving care. I gave myself to her absolutely.

# 9

Towards nine o'clock the next evening, a dying summer's evening, another still evening when the electric light is switched on but seems to burn darker than usual, we sat together in silence over a cold supper. We sat in our accustomed places, myself at the head of the table looking straight out over the garden, Madge at one side with the plates and dishes before her. Cold mutton, radishes and lettuce, the pale finger of cheese lying ready at the side. The bread stood dryly by itself, the light tried without success to draw a glint of life from a square, mustard-thick chutney bottle.

All day we had dropped into such silences. She had tried to talk of it, to find out what had been happening to me. She had made no complaint whatsoever—only once, but in rumination, she had wondered aloud what had made me so distrust her after so many years. I wanted to cry. To this tenderness I could answer little, shaking my head rather and breaking off when I started somehow to try and explain what was, obviously, so reasonless. I had shaken my head and stopped, muttering always that a little later, a little later, I would say. Then silence, as we both thought.

Madge explained, and apologized, for that kiss. It had been in fun, it was wrong—she saw that—but still it had been only fun. It had been the evening and the party, the spirit of it. It had been the first time, and for her part certainly the last: it had meant so little that she had not thought much about it at all. To this I could only nod, deeply I felt the tenderness with which she tried to explain. But again silence—there was nothing to do or say, the event was over and it was not even worthwhile being wise after it. I felt the negative, neutral, neither lost nor found but absolutely inactive sensation a man might feel who, after a life of activity, has suffered some shattering and sobering loss or illness, destroying a lifetime's habit, leaving him no reason to act whatever in any way. For what would be the use?

Thus the day. But as the physical signs of my distress became less apparent, as that danger receded, and as from my silences her intuition had gathered for herself part of the story, Madge had not remained purely tender. So far she had said nothing. But in her face, as sometimes across the table she looked at me, I caught from time to time a reflective and secret glint of amusement, something amusing to herself from which she seemed to gather nourishment.

All those cold things on the table stood still. They stood dead on the white tablecloth that in its damask showed a starchy life, a field of white cloth a little stained with old gravy. With the picnic on Sunday, it had not been changed.

I looked down at this cloth, seeing it, thinking. Thoughts that seemed so unworthwhile they were never finished—these drifted recurrently, weakly, none worth a tremor of concern. Norma dead. Charley dying. Did I

mind whether Charley died, or whether he lived? What if
Charley died? What if Charley lived? Would it matter?
I had wanted him, but now that would be useless, if he
came back there would be nothing to want. Nor nothing
to want him to die for. Forever after, what would, what
*could* happen? And Madge there, Madge who had been so
understanding, would she ever be quite the same? Would
not some seed of distrust always lie between us, waiting
always to quicken? Could either of us really trust the
other as we had done before? I sat there in the dark electric light. An ill man from whom the illness had been
purged, I was void.

In the deepening evening, a white plume of smoke rose
from the round brick ventilator, hovered down an instant
over the wistaria, wreathed away dissembling into clear
still air. As it had done in the past, as it would continue
to do for many, many days to come.